Reckless Intentions
BY: Adrianne L. Cunningham

Cunningham, Adrianne

Reckless Intention Adrianne L. Cunningham – 1st Ed.

First Paperback Edition © 2014

Publisher: Black Destiny Publications

PRINTED IN THE UNITED STATES OF AMERICA

ACKNOWLEDGEMENTS

I want to first and foremost give all praises to God for granting me the gift and talent to write. Without Him none of this would be possible.

I would also like to thank my family and friends (Kentucky, Alabama, Tennessee, New York and Michigan) for their undying support and faith in me to get this book finished. I hope you find this book insightful and with a distinct message.

CHAPTER ONE

"Damn," I shouted, as I felt the tears welling up. My eyes felt like they were on fire. I was trying to stay focused as I flew down the highway—in the pouring rain—without a license. "I can't lose her, not now and not ever!"

***

I remember the very first time I saw her—it was the spring of 2004; I will never forget that day. It was a Saturday, around 8:00 am; my cousin's car had finally fucked up on him, his brakes were wailing. Mooch had an old '76 Coupe; it was his baby, and he loved to floss it on some rims. Screeching all the way, we made it to Uncle Brutus' Auto Shop. Mooch and I were sitting outside the shop, smoking a cigarette, when we heard a car with a rattling and raggedy muffler headed our way.

"Damn dude, somebody's car needs more work than mine." Mooch started laughing.

A grey Camry with tinted windows was pulling up beside us. The noise was so loud, that it gave me a headache. I couldn't imagine driving around town with that shit.

"Finally. I'm glad they cut that off; it was making my head pound," Cuz whispered.

I shook my head; I felt sorry for that person because that shit had to be embarrassing. I nearly dropped my cigarette when I saw a beautiful, honey-brown chick with long black hair, titties like melons just right for grabbing, and thick in all the right places, step out of her ride. All I could think to myself was Thank you God. She was on the phone, arguing with someone on the other end.

"Look, I 'ma call you back," she snapped.

Those glossy and luscious lips turned up in a disgusted smirk as she struggled to get something out of the backseat. She hung up the phone, and tossed it in her bag, obviously annoyed.

When she emerged from the car, she was carrying an adorable little girl. She was a little darker than her mom, but equally as beautiful. Her long black pigtails swayed from side to side as her mother picked her up. She looked just like an angel.

"Isis—girl, wake up." she said softly, as she kissed and hugged the little girl before she put her down gently. The sleepy toddler held her mom's hand as they walked in our direction. I felt my heart pounding at every step she took. Even though she was irritated, I immediately wanted to approach her. I stretched out my arm, and made my way back to the front door of the auto shop.

"Good morning ladies. Let me get the door for you."

My suave moves always seemed to work and get a smile out of the ladies. Every woman wanted to feel special and beautiful. Yes, I know about the ladies— so much so, that they love to put their babies on me. They did it just to have a reason to call me, or hope that I give them some of this eight-inch pipe. Am I just being cocky by braggin' on my piece? Maybe, but the truth is that women love it big. They may say that size doesn't matter but that's bullshit. It matters— please believe it.

"Thank you," the little girl said, as she smiled and waved at me.

"Yes, thanks." The mother gave me a smile that gave me an erection. Her eyes and her lips almost had me losing my mind.

"You're so very welcome." I licked my lips and headed in behind them; I felt like a lion on the prowl. With this chick, I was not taking no for an answer.

Little Isis tugged on her mom's shirttail. "Mommy, is this man gonna make your car sound better?"

I ducked my head and smiled.

"Yes baby." She laughed.

They made their way to the counter. Damn, I wish I could have been those Baby Phat jeans she was wearing. That back end was looking ripe.

"Welcome to Brutus', do you have an appointment?" my aunt Ann asked with a smile.

"Yes ma'am, I was supposed to be here at eight a.m., and I'm sorry for being a little late."

"It's ok sweetie. My son will be up here shortly to get your keys and move your car." My aunt looked down at the little girl who was smiling.

"Oh great, thanks." She sighed in relief.

"Go to the waiting area, right there where my nephew is sitting; when I come back, I will find some homemade chocolate chip cookies and a Disney movie." My aunt must have been looking out for me that day; I think she saw what I saw in this woman.

"Yippee," Isis shouted.

"I think you won my baby over."

"What's your name, sweet pea?" My aunt knelt down and smiled at Isis.

"My name is Isis Lashay Williams and I am almost three years old." She held up three fingers and smiled at her accomplishment. Her mother and Aunt Ann laughed in amazement.

"And when is your birthday, Isis?" Aunt Ann said smiling.

"My birthday is August 7th."

"Well sweetie, you have a little while. Would you like to walk back here with me? We can get the cookies and the movie." My aunt grinned, and stretched out her hand.

"Can I Mommy?" Isis rocked from side to side, looking at her mom for approval.

"Be my guest. Oh, and Isis, please don't be asking a whole lot of questions."

"Ok Mommy!" Isis and my aunt walked to the back of the shop.

The vision of loveliness headed in my direction, and sat two chairs down from me.

"Hello again." I smiled and looked over her body from head to toe.

"I guess so," she sighed, and managed to put on a smile.

"My name is Yung." I reached out to shake her hand. I had to get into swagger mode for this one. This chick set my soul on fire.

She accepted my handshake and laughed. "Yung— really? I seriously doubt that name is on your birth certificate."

I loved the way she smiled.

"Well, my real name is Victor, but people call me Yung—" I trailed off because this girl had me speechless.

"Ok well, my name is Chante; but people call me Chante." We both laughed.

"I see you got jokes; I just want you to know—I think you are beautiful!" I looked into her eyes, and gave her a sly grin.

By the bored look on her face, I could tell that she really wasn't impressed. A chick like her was probably used to pick up lines.

"Really—is that the best you can do?"

"I wasn't trying to be funny; I really think you are beautiful. I would love the chance to get to know you, if you decide to let me into your world."

I gave her my 'I'm serious' look; women love it when a man isn't afraid to show how they really feel. And boom, just like that, I'd laid the trap out.

"That's new." She shook her head.

"So tell me; do you have a man, Ms. Lady?"

She hesitated for a moment or two; I figured she was about to tell me she was taken.

"No, not really," she sighed. "I just have a baby daddy."

"Oh, so y'all still be talking?"

"No," she blurted out. She rolled her eyes and said, "But you know how some guys only wanna come around when they feel there is a new player in the game."

"Oh I see."

I totally understood. Shit, if I had a baby momma that fine, I would stay on her too. "I guess some men are afraid to admit they lost out on a good thing. But it's like they say, 'One man's loss is another man's gain'—right?

"Uh huh, I can see your point."

I could tell from her expression that she still thought I was feeding her another line.

"Seriously Chante, I meant no disrespect."

"You're straight, Yung." She giggled.

"Ok, I'm gonna hit you with my number."

I dug in my pockets, found an old receipt in my pocket, and grabbed one of the pens sitting on the newspaper stand. I smiled, as I wrote my number down and handed it to her.

"I hope you decide to give me a call. What phone service do you have? Cellphone, I mean?"

9

"Oh," she smiled "I have AT&T."

"Word? Me too! So we can talk for free!"

That's truly amazing." She looked at me and grinned sarcastically.

"I'm just saying; we wouldn't have to talk at a certain time, because it's free regardless."

"I feel you," she murmured. She looked at her nails, still unimpressed.

"Why don't you go ahead and dial my number, and I can save you in my phone."

She looked a little dazed, but pulled out her white iPhone and dialed my number. I smiled with total satisfaction when I saw her number come through. I immediately entered 'My Boo' as her contact name, without putting a lot of thought into it.

"I got you in there, so don't be afraid to use that number."

She laughed slightly, looked me over and said, "you either."

I was blown away! I was giving her the gangster and she was giving it back; I loved that! We sat for an instant just gazing at each other. I wondered what she was thinking. I wanted to climb over the seat and attack her sexy ass!

"Yung!"

I snapped out of the trance that Chante had cast on me.

"Whassup, Cuz?"

I turned in Mooch's direction and I could see him checking Chante out. Honestly, I was getting pissed. I couldn't blame my cuz for admiring her though; she was such a beautiful woman.

"Unc said he is through with the brakes, let's bounce." He motioned to the front door.

"Well Ms. Chante, it's been a pleasure meeting you."

I stood up, grabbed her hand, and lightly kissed it. My eyes never lost focus of hers.

"Oh thank you, kind sir," she said softly, and blushed a little bit.

"Hit me up when you have the time," I added.

Chante nodded and replied, "Well, if I take too long to call, maybe you can call me."

I laughed, but nodded in agreement.

As I headed to the door, I turned back and told her, "I will talk to you a little later."

Satisfied—yeah, I think that's the best word to describe how I felt at that moment.

"Snap out of it Cuz, I'm trying to talk to you." Mooch yelled; he was such a hater. .

"Man, what's up?" I was annoyed because he broke me out of my reverie.

"What about Marcie?"

Why was this dude bringing up that trifling trick in this conversation?

"What about that bitch?"

Marcie, was my ex, and for a good reason. .I was drunk at a Christmas party, and she looked alright; need I say more? The past year had been bullshit; I wish I'd never run up on her. You never pick the girl you hit on the first day to be wifey! Shit, if I got it that easy, so could the next man. And to top it all off, now the bitch is trying to put her eight-week-old son on me man, I still sexed her every now and then, but even she said I wasn't the only guy.

"You know how it is, that chick be acting stupid." Mooch said, laughing.

My temper was rising; I wasn't trying to hear that bullshit.

11

"Exactly, and I'm not with her stupid ass, so drop it."

Mooch looked at me, and wisely let the conversation end.

"My fault, Cuz. So what's the status on baby girl from the shop?"

"It's on, Mooch, this one is a keeper," I said proudly, and gave him dap.

"What? Yeah, right."

"I'm telling you, that chick is definitely gonna be Mrs. DaMone."

Mooch cranked up the music and laughed as we drove through the city. He thought I was running game, but I was dead serious.

***

We made it to the South Side Slums, better known as the "PJ's". I was glad to be getting out of the car, because Cuz spent the majority of the ride telling lies about all the women he supposedly banged in his ride. I know he loves to lie, but I wondered if he cleaned out his seats; I didn't want to be sitting in dried-up nut stains.

"I'm telling you, Yung, that girl was a pro!"

"I feel ya man." I tried to sound interested, but I hoped he was through.

"So what we got up for tonight?" Mooch always looked to me to get the party going but right now, that was the last thing on my mind.

I took a deep breath, sighed, and responded, "I don't know, I'm gonna see whassup wit sexy from the shop.

"Damn, you're not sprung already, are you?" Mooch said, rolling his eyes at me.

I didn't bother responding to that bull he was on. What was the point? Mooch and I shared a two bedroom, one bath bachelor pad; I was gonna have to hear his mouth regardless.

Mooch pulled out his phone and started scrolling.

"I'm gonna get one of my chicks in route. Might wanna have a little fun at noon time, ya dig?"

"I hear ya," I laughed. Those young hood rats he dealt with were definitely beneath me. Mooch was twenty-four, and talking to young, dumb college chicks. You know the kind, those "gGirls gone wild type chicks" that you really can't take home to meet your mom.

"If it don't work out with ol' girl, you want me to hook you up?"

"Come on now, I'm on my big boy shit; I ain't got time for the minor leagues. You do you." I snapped at him, feeling very insulted.

"Whatever." Mooch threw his hand up; he dialed a number and headed into his room.

I made my way through our pad. Our black and brown living room setuite had a wrap-around black leather couch. We'd hung a red strobe light over it, which killed it. We also had a sixty-inch plasma TV with surround sound; adding a little extra flavor. There was a nice little bar set up by the kitchen entrance; convenient for making our dates' drinks while they were sitting at the bar—talk about smooth. I couldn't wait to invite Chante over! I fixed myself a ham and cheese sandwich, found some Gatorade and made my way to the couch. I didn't want to seem too anxious, but I wanted to call Chante right away. It had been a couple hours since we met, but I couldn't get her off my mind.

Ring! Ring!

I felt my heart pounding, but soon realized it was only Marcie calling.

13

"What?" I sighed.

"Damn, why you gotta answer the phone like that?" Marcie asked, while smacking in my ear.

"What do you want?" I snarled; my blood was boiling. The sooner I got this trick off the phone, the sooner I could call Chante.

"Uggh, I just wanted to know if you wanted to go to Malik's doctor appointment tomorrow?"

"Really?" I just shook my head and laughed. This chick will try anything to get around me and it's sad.

"Yes really. It's tomorrow at 10 a.m."

"I doubt that lil' girl." I continued to laugh at her stupidity.

"What you mean?"

"Tomorrow is Sunday, dummy! I'm busy, so next time, get your lies straight!"

"Look—"

I hung up on her ass. She called back three times, and the last time left a message, I figured that ought to free me up for at least an hour or two.

I found Chante's number and immediately pressed the send button. To my surprise, she answered on the third ring.

"Hello Yung."

"I see you remembered my name." I felt special at that moment.

"Yeah, I guess I did."

I breathed a sigh of relief. "You were taking too long to call, so I figured I would call you."

"I'm sorry; I'm at work, but I'm on my break right now."

"Oh ok." I felt a little better knowing she was working, and hadn't just forgotten about me.

"Yeah, so what's up?" she replied.

"I been thinking about you since earlier this morning. I wanted to talk to you and see if we could meet up later on today."

"Wow, you don't waste any time. In fact, you have perfect timing. I get off in a few hours and my daughter is gone for the rest of the weekends. She is staying with her grandma."

"So I guess you are free?" I felt victorious.

"I guess so."

I sat there with so many thoughts running through mind. "I tell you what; give me a call after you have had time to get home and relax. Can you do that for me?"

"I will definitely think it over."

"Well sweetheart, I don't want to take up too much of your break, but be sure to call me and we can meet up."

"Alright."

"I can't wait." I smiled.

"I bet; goodbye Yung."

"Oh no, sweetie, we never say goodbye; it's see you later."

"Ok then, see you later."

"You bet."

Chapter Two

I was patiently waiting for Chante to give me a call. It's sad to say, but I couldn't seem to get that girl out of my head.

"Yung!" She yelled in the phone.

Uggh, my momma be killing me sometimes, like I'm her only child. It's four of us and I'm the only son. But that's how I got put on point with the ladies, being around nothing but women.

"Yes Momma."

"Can you go to the store and get me a pack of cigarettes and a two liter of Pepsi?"

Damn, here we go with this shit again, I thought to myself.

"Mom, you know I'm way across town. Where is Shannon or April?"

"Boy, they got their kids and other stuff to worry about. April's car needs to be fixed. You better get your butt over here, and don't make me have to call you back."

Momma hung up the phone. I'm pretty sure my sisters are just sitting at Momma's doing nothing. The store is right up the street from them, it's not like they can't walk. But it's been like this ever since I was little.

My parents got married at a young age, they were childhood sweethearts. My mom found out she was pregnant with my oldest sister, Amari, and dropped out of school at seventeen. I was next and then came the twins; Shannon and April. Times really got tough after my dad left when I was around ten years old. Amari was thirteen, so the twins were about six years old at that time. That's a lot for one black woman, but my mom managed with the help of our family.

Even though he left the house, Pops would still come around for us kids. Amari has never forgiven him for leaving, but the rest of us are cool with him. I used to get mad because I didn't want to be "the man of the house" at a young age. But I guess it helped to make me a stronger man.

My phone rang, and startled me; it was my mom calling back.

"I'm on the way Momma."

"Well, you need to hurry up," she said, and hung up again. I swear my momma is the only woman that can cuss me out. I stopped by the store, got my mom's things and rode down the street to her house. I wish my mom would think about painting her two-story home another color. It's been light purple ever since we were kids. My mom still had my room the same way I left it four years back. She was mad at me for moving out, but a man needs his own space. I got tired of bringing chicks to my mom's house. I was nineteen when I moved out.

I opened the purple painted door. I could smell fried chicken and greens coming from the kitchen. Mom stayed on point; I'd come at the right time.

"It took you long enough," my mom snapped. She stood there, all five foot three inches of her. Mom was short, and heavyset, but when she put her hands on her hips, you knew she meant business.

"I love you too Momma," I mumbled, putting the cigarettes on the kitchen table and the Pepsi in the fridge.

"Uh huh," she grunted.

"Dang bruh, you didn't bring me anything?" April was always complaining or whining about something.

17

She must have lost her mind, I thought. Before I knew it, I yelled, "Don't start; you could've walked your lazy ass to the store and I wouldn't have had to drive all the way over here!"

"Excuse me? My son is asleep and Momma said she didn't want to watch him." April rolled her eyes so hard; I wondered why they didn't get stuck in that position.

"You could've put him in the stroller I bought him. You are just lazy, girl. You're probably waiting on your child support check in the mail."

"You know it," she winked and returned to the living room.

I shook my head, turned around and asked, "Momma, why don't you make April do anything around here?"

"Boy, don't you start with me." Momma raised her hand like she was going to hit me. "Are you hungry?"

"You know I can eat," I replied, and we both laughed.

"So where have you been hiding? I haven't seen you in a week." She was at the stove fixing my plate, and my mouth was watering. Moms could throw down on some good ol' stick to your ribs, soul food.

"Come on now, I was just over here Tuesday."

"That's a long time."

Again we laughed. My sisters could stay gone for days at a time, but I had to check in on a daily basis.

I paused, and lit a cigarette. "I met someone today; I think she is the one."

"Oh really? Am I gonna get to meet this one?" Momma sat my steaming hot food in front of me; she reached for the ashtray, and stubbed her cigarette butt out.

"Ha ha, very funny," I grinned. "Now, what's that supposed to mean?'

"I'm your momma, but you will take them girls around everyone but me." Momma put her hands on her hips.

"Aw, is my favorite girl getting jealous? That's only because some of them girls were not good enough to meet you, Ma. Only the best for you." I walked over to my mom and gave her a kiss on the cheek.

"Uh huh," she looked me up and down with a sarcastic smirk. "So, will I get to meet the mystery woman?"

"Yea Momma, you will definitely get to meet Chante Morgan."

"Oh I see; you must really like her. I have never seen you light up like that before."

"I'm telling you Mom, she is the one."

"Uh huh, I will be the judge of that."

Shannon came bursting into the room, asking "What are you talking about, Ma?"

She ran up to me and gave me a hug. We were the closest in the family. I respected her and she respected me. I was proud of her because she was going to community college, and doing something productive with herself.

"Your brother thinks he has found the right one," Momma mumbled, all frowned up.

"For real? Good for you bruh, it's about time." Shannon smiled showing her dimples.

I just nodded in agreement. Since I was thirteen, I'd been spitting game to the ladies. I see through all their sob stories and I see that there's no truth in them. Trying to run game on me because they think I'm just young, dumb and full of—well, you know. But I swear, when I look into a woman's eyes, I can just see their bullshit. That's why I hold my heart very carefully, because a trick is not going to destroy me. But I looked into Chante's eyes and I saw purity in her spirit. In my heart, I felt that she would not and could not destroy me. I saw the hurt in her eyes. If she would let me love her; I'd show her things that she never thought imaginable.

"Dang bruh, you were daydreaming big time; Ms. Thang got you like that, huh?" Shannon was giggling.

Shannon was my ace in the hole and we have always been close. We are a lot alike. Baby sis likes to play the "innocent little school girl" role, but she be pimpin'. But, unlike her twin or as I call her, Easy Go, she makes sure she protects herself from pregnancy.

"What you talkin' bout girl?" I was a little dazed.

"I been trying to get your attention for a couple minutes now."

"Oh." I rubbed my head, like I always did when I felt embarrassed.

Shannon patted me on the shoulder. "Do we need to talk?"

"Maybe so, Baby Gangster."

I patted my head, and pondered for a minute. I needed to get a woman's perspective on the situation, because I had never really felt these feelings before. Plus, I know whatever I discuss with Shannon will stay between us.

"Hey Uncle Vic." My three year old nephew, Ricardo ran full speed ahead, and jumped in my lap. Ricardo was a result of a six month love affair with a twenty-five year old divorced military sergeant, Ricardo Lopez. Rick didn't know my "hot in the ass" little sister was only fifteen at the time, because she had lied about her age.

20

He still has problems with her lies and deception. We talk from time to time, and apparently he loves my little sister. Rick said that even though she lied, he will forgive her. Rick is Catholic and believes he has to work things out with the mother of his child. He really spoils them.

"Whassup nephew?" I smiled, as Ricardo ran into my arms.

"Where have you been?" He wrapped his little arms around my neck and hugged tight.

"Boy, you are worse than your grandma."

"He has probably been with some skanky chic." April managed to weasel her way into the conversation, rolling her eyes at all of us. Although April and Shannon were identical twins, they were as different as night and day.

"I couldn't have been with the skanks. All your friends were on their knees with other niggas."

"Boy please, you are the whore. You slept with all of my close friends. Now half of them aren't even cool with one another." She looked offended.

April looked offended, and her lip was stuck out.

"Easy come, easy go." I smiled.

"Uggh. I hate you." April grabbed her son by the arm, and headed to the bathroom.

"I love you too." I loved to make her angry.

"You two stay into it." Shannon took a bottle of water from the fridge.

"Naw, she stays into it, that's just how she shows her affection," I smiled. April always has to play the hard role. She has got it made. She gets money from Rick, and he bought her a 2009 Dodge Charger. April has never worked for anything, but she is always complaining about something.

I gave Shannon some dap. "You got your school money, a part-time job, and you're making things happen. I'm proud of you sis."

"Thanks. We need to ride out and talk though."

I knew what that meant, so I hurried and finished my food. I told Momma that I would see her later. Shannon decided we would ride in her car; it was better on gas. I loved the tint on her dark blue Camry because it was right at the legal limit and no one could see in the windows at night. I pulled my 2000 cherry red Suburban with the peanut butter interior, up into Momma's carport and headed to Shannon's ride. I liked her matching interior with the Sponge Bob theme. Her car always smelled like coconut or cherry blunt spray.

"So what's on your mind, sis?"

I saw her reach in her ashtray for the White Owl that was rolled. Shannon handed it to me.

"Nothing, but the best for our talks." She smiled as she drove off.

" Whassup." I lit the Owl and coughed.

"I'm thinking about moving out of Momma's by the summer."

"I feel you."

"Yeah, me and Devin were thinking about getting a place. I would rather have my own place and let him come over."

"Oh, so you don't want to commit?" I was surprised at what she said, because most chicks seem to like having a man around.

"I don't want to share a lease with him because we could break up, and that could be ugly."

"Ok, I see what you are saying. I think you might have the right idea."

She passed the Owl. "We're gonna split the bills, but I'm gonna get the apartment in my name. I know that with or without him, I can afford it."

"That's good Baby Gangster."

I was proud of the way she was thinking. Shannon and Amari had goals and always stuck to their principles. Amari was married with two kids in South Carolina. We were in North Carolina and Momma didn't like the distance. But Amari's husband, Sergeant Malcolm Richmond, was stationed there for the moment. To top it off, he happens to know Ricardo. Malcolm didn't know that April was seeing Rick until it was too late. She had been careful enough not to go places that Malcolm would be.

"Yea, Momma's gonna be mad." She took a couple pulls from the Owl.

"No doubt! I left the house four years ago and Momma is still pissed."

I knew that conversation wasn't gonna go well. Two of her kids had already left the nest. "But you gotta live for yourself, Shannon. Momma knows we love her but we gotta leave the nest at some point in time."

"That's because you are her baby boy!" Shannon reached over and pinched my cheek; I could tell that she was buzzing. We rode to Eastland Park, one of my favorite places. I enjoyed sitting on the park benches there to clear my mind.

"So whassup with you, bruh?" She directed the conversation back to me. We sat across from each other on the bench.

"Sis, the girl I met today—oh my God." I pulled out a cigarette and lit it, and then I bowed my head.

"Bruh, you just met her today."

23

"I have never had these feelings before, but they came up when I saw her and talked to her," I breathed a deep sigh, still imagining her smile and laugh.

Shannon popped a stick of gum in her mouth before she murmured, "I definitely got to meet this chick. I have never heard you talk like this."

"That's what I'm saying. I'm waiting on her to call me when she gets off from work." I flicked my cigarette ashes and took another pull; I felt anxiety building up in my chest.

"What time does she get off?"

"She gets off at 6 p.m.I told her to call me when she got home and relaxed for a little while." What I really meant was bathed, perfumed, and looking sexy for me!

"She should be calling any minute now; you want me to take you back to your car?" Shannon rose to her feet and grabbed her keys.

I hesitated for a moment before answering; this chick gave me butterflies. I raised an eyebrow and gazed intensely at my sister.

"Maybe you could ride with me."

"Dang, she must be super bad—just like me."

We both laughed, but it was true.

Chapter Three

I'm glad Shannon agreed to hang with me. I'm serious about this girl, but I wanted see if my sister gets the same positive vibe from her. Chante called around 6:45 p.m. I told her that I was on the way over to her house with my sister. Surprisingly, when she gave me her address, I found out that Chante only stayed four blocks over from me. This is definitely a plus. Shannon pulled up into the Wingate Apartments. We found apartment 112.

"Are you ready to meet my angel?" I was smiling from ear to ear.

"I guess so." Shannon patted me on the back, as I knocked on Chante's apartment door.

"Whassup Yung?" Chante opened the door wearing a blue and grey sundress, which showed her lovely caramel legs. I loved the way her breasts slightly bulged out of her strapless dress. Her hair hung down to her shoulders.

"Hello beautiful, this is my baby sister, Shannon." I said softly, and kissed her hand.

"Nice to meet you, Shannon." Chante extended her hand to my sister.

"Likewise, I heard a lot about you today."

I rolled my eyes and raised an eyebrow at Shannon.

"I hope they were all good things," Chante looked at me with a sympathetic glance.

"Of course, only good things about you, ma'am."

We entered her apartment that was decorated in beige and lavender. Momma would love it over here. Could this be a sign?

Shannon looked around, and exclaimed, "Wow! Momma would love this. Purple is her favorite color."

"Really?" Chante grinned.

Shannon giggled. "Yeah, our crib is purple with a purple door."

Chante chuckled. "I might like it over there too."

"That can be arranged—if you wanna go over there." I gently caressed her soft cheek, steadily keeping eye contact.

"Are you always this smooth?" She blushed.

Chante invited us into the living room. There was incense burning and a movie was playing on the television.

"Would you two like anything to drink or eat?"

"What do you have?" I replied.

"Soda, water or a Bud Light."

"I'm not sure; can I come in the kitchen and decide for myself?"

"Sure; would you like anything, Shannon?"

"A soda will be fine. I will sit here and wait for you guys to bring it back from the kitchen."

We all laughed while Chante led the way.

"Get what you want," She pointed to the drinks.

I looked in the fridge and then looked back at her.

"But what if I want something that isn't in the fridge?"

I came in close to her. I wrapped one arm gently around her waist and looked deep into her eyes.

"And what do you want, Yung?"

"That's easy; I want you." I whispered in her ear.

I gently kissed the outside of her soft and tender ear, and slowly brought my face directly in front of hers. She began to bite her bottom lip. Apparently her ear was a sensitive spot.

"I want to love you, if you will let me." I instantly began to feel my nature rise.

"You just met me today," she sighed.

"I feel like this is love at first sight."

26

I slowly placed my hand across her heart. It was beating strong.

"Your heart is beating just as fast as mine; maybe you can give me a chance."

I couldn't wait any longer; I leaned in, and we kissed. I sucked on her lower lip and slid my tongue in her ready and wet mouth. I wrapped my arms around her slim waist. Her body was accepting of mine. I ran my fingers over her hardened nipples and heard her whimper.

"Boy stop, I'm getting outside of myself right now. I just met you."

I smiled, even though I didn't want that feeling to end.

"But the heart doesn't lie. I respect you and I wouldn't feel right about anything more than kissing right now."

"That's good to know," she whispered, and straightened out her dress.

"I demand respect. I'm not trying to go through no bull, not anymore."

"I hear you sweet lady. There's nothing wrong with kissing. I would love to kiss you some more." I kissed her hand and looked deep into her eyes

"We'll have to see about that; but right now, I'm sure your sister is waiting on her soda."

"Yeah, I guess you're right." I said, even though I was a little disappointed.

We made our way back to the living room. Shannon was flipping through one of the photo albums that Chante had on her coffee table.

"I hope you don't mind me looking through your pictures?" Shannon said.

"No, I don't mind." Chante shook her head.

"You have a beautiful little girl."

27

"Uh huh," I said in agreement, and made my way to the sofa.

"I met little Isis this morning. She was at Unc's auto shop with her momma."

"Oh ok," Shannon snickered.

"That daughter of mine is really something else," Chante laughed.

"This has to be her daddy," Shannon stated as she turned to a picture of a dark-skinned, tall and muscular dude. He was wearing a black fitted cap over some cornrows, with a wife-beater and slacks. Isis was in his arms smiling.

"Yea." Chante rolled her eyes.

"I think you struck a nerve, sis." I smiled at Chante.

"It's ok." Chante shrugged and brushed it off.

"My baby looks just like him and there's no denying that. Despite our failed relationship, he is a great father. So that's the most important thing."

"Oh; does he come by very often?" Shannon asked the obvious question, because she saw me feeling uneasy.

"Sometimes. He's doing better about calling first though."

"So he likes to pop up on you?" I felt uneasy asking her that, but I had to know. I didn't want to have to whoop his behind if he came at me wrong.

"Sometimes, he does; although I don't think he will today since Isis is with him. That fool will probably call though." Chante was starting to look irritated, and it resonated in her voice

"Sounds like he doesn't want to let you go, and honestly I can't blame him."

Chante was blushing; she looked over at my sister and said, "Shannon, does your brother always talk like this?"

Shannon's phone began to ring before she had a chance to answer.

"Yes ma'am. I'm with Yung right now; I don't know—hold on," Shannon handed me the phone.

"Hello Momma."

"Don't hello me, what are y'all doing?" Momma killed me with her attitude

"We are just hanging out Ma."

"Uh huh," Momma cleared her throat.

"I thought you were meeting that Chante girl? I guess she never called you."

"We are over at her house right now."

"What? Put me on speakerphone, Victor Quincy DaMone." Momma screamed so loud that everyone heard it

I hesitated. It's not that serious. But, I did it anyway, because you didn't tell Momma no.

"Hello Chante." My momma put on a pleasant voice.

"Hello," Chante replied.

"I'm Victor's momma." "How are you, Mrs. DaMone?" Chante seemed surprised.

"Well, I see she has manners. That's a plus." Momma giggled.

Shannon let out a laugh.

"Shut up, Shan. I just wanted to know when I might get to meet you, since everyone else already has."

"Umm, I'm sure we will meet soon," I could see the desperation in Chante's eyes.

"Uh huh, what are you doing tomorrow at 5:00 p.m.?"

29

"I don't have any plans ma'am."

"She's so polite." Momma laughed, and continued her semi-interrogation.

"Well, would you like to come over for dinner?"

"You don't have to if you don't want to." I tried to whisper.

"Boy shut up. I was not talking to you." Momma hollered.

"That would be fine, Mrs. DaMone." Chante winked at me.

"Ok, I will see you at 5 p.m., tomorrow." Momma returned to her pleasant voice

"Yes ma'am. Looking forward to it."

"Likewise Shan, you need to get over here. Devin is on the way over, he called the house phone." Momma responded.

"Ok Momma. I guess we gotta get ready to go. It was nice to meet you Chante."

"Yes it was." Chante rose to her feet.

"Damn, I wasn't ready to go yet, but I gotta go get my ride from my mom's."

"It's cool." Chante patted me on the back.

"Naw. Would you like to ride with us to go get my ride?" I was still not ready to leave her.

"Yea, ride with us but stay in the car because my momma will talk you to death." Shannon smiled.

We all laughed.

"Sure. She was gonna see me tomorrow anyways."

We made our way to Shannon's car. I was so excited just being around Chante and I didn't know why. Chante immediately sat in Shannon's backseat and I decided to join her.

"Damn! Am I supposed to be your taxi?"

"Shut up sis. Pass me that White Owl." I frowned.

"I didn't know y'all smoked." Chante looked a little surprised.

"Yes honey and on a regular," Shannon nodded. "We could have smoked in my house. That's why I was burning the incense."

"Hmm. Great minds think alike." I passed the White Owl to her, carefully placing my hand on her thigh. I couldn't resist touching her and wanting to explore even more. Chante passed it to Shannon. I whispered in her ear that I wanted to 'explore'. I placed my jacket on her lap so Shannon could not see my hand movements.

"So, where do you work?"

"Oh...ummm...I work for UPS." Chante was distracted because my fingers had found their way to her panty line.

"True, that's whassup." Shannon nodded.

Shannon blasted a song that was on the radio as I continued to explore. Slipping my fingers inside her panties, I felt Chante's shaven and wet pussy. With every bump in the road, I felt her body quiver. I found her clit and massaged it with my index finger. She tried to keep a straight face but when she climaxed it was hard to play that off. I know how to please a woman.

"Are you ok back there? You might not want to pull on that White Owl too hard," she laughed.

Chante blushed as she gazed over at me. I slowly removed my hand from under her dress. Never losing eye contact, I placed my index finger in my mouth to taste her sweetness. Just as I thought, she tasted like sugar. I couldn't wait to put my mouth where my finger was.

"To be continued." I whispered in her ear.

"I think that was bad enough." She breathed in my ear.

"Only respectful things. I told you I would only kiss you right now but I didn't say where." I whispered.

"We are here." Shannon replied.

Both Chante and I snapped out of our fantasy world in the backseat.

"Yep, let's make a run for it."

"I don't mind going in there and speaking to your mom. I mean, I am at her house."

"No. Trust me. She will have plenty of time to drill you with questions tomorrow."

Shannon nodded her head in agreement. I didn't see my mom's car in the garage, so it was the perfect time to vamp. I said my goodbyes to my sister and we left.

"You really have a nice ride." Chante was getting a feel for my leather interior.

"Thank you ma'am." I winked.

"No problem." She giggled and looked over her face in the mirror she took from her purse.

"You really felt good. Do you taste as good as you feel?" I licked my lips.

"Huh?" Chante looked surprised.

"Was that too much to ask?"

"It did catch me off guard."

"I'm sorry."

"It's ok." She shook her head. "But to answer your question, I don't know."

"Are you going to let me find out?"

"I just met you."

"I know sweetie, I told you no sex. I just want to explore you with my mouth."

"Wow."

I laughed. If she thought my fingers were something, she probably can't handle my tongue.

"I really don't know how to respond to that." Chante replied as she rolled down her window. "I'm not used to a guy asking me that on the first date."

"I can understand, I believe in going on how I feel. That's why I approached you this morning. I saw a diamond and I wanted it."

"Oh really. So you just want to sleep with me?" She seemed upset

"No sweetie, I want all of you but I would be lying if I said you didn't turn me on."

Her phone began to ring and from the look on her face I could tell it was not someone she wanted to talk to.

"Hello. Oh, hi sweetie...love you too. No, I don't need to speak to your daddy...ok. See you on Monday." She sounded dry

"Must've been Isis." I was relieved there was no drama.

"Yea, she likes to call me. That girl loves to talk!" She smiled.

"I can't wait to have some kids. I guess I just haven't been with the right person yet."

"Enjoy your freedom while it lasts." She grinned.

"I guess so. There's a girl who is trying to put her baby on me but we are scheduled to get a blood test in a few weeks."

"Do you think it's yours?"

"I'm not sure, but if it is, I will take responsibility."

"Well that's good."

I pulled up to Chante's apartment. She fumbled around for her keys and then we made our way inside her place.

"So tell me Chante, what do you look for in a man?"

She sat down beside me and pulled out a swisher that was already rolled and lit it.

"Honesty and maturity."

"Is that all?"

"Those are the main things."

"So Isis' daddy didn't have either of those qualities?"

"No. He likes to play games and cheat. But he always expected me to just sit around and wait on him." She laughed

"How long have you two been broken up?"

"Over a year now." She passed the swisher to me.

"I just couldn't take it anymore. I'm twenty-four and I don't have time for his mess."

"I hear you. I'm twenty-three but I want someone real and I think you're the realest."

"Really?" She smiled.

"Yes really, let me show you."

I laid her back, making sure she had a pillow under her head.

I kissed her neck. "Chante," you just don't know what you do to me and I can't explain it but I love it."

I made my way down her chest with my tongue. She liked it. She opened her legs and wrapped them around my waist.

"Promise me that you will respect me in the morning." She moaned.

"I will. I told you no sex and I meant that." I raised up her dress

I gently kissed her belly button and made my way to her inner thigh. I could feel her body start to quiver and her hips moved from side to side. I slid her panties down and saw that hot, pretty, pink pussy. My mouth began to water. At first, I gently kissed her pussy lips. I felt her hands massaging my head and that turned me on even more.

"Do you like this?" I asked.

She moaned as her response. I began inserting one and then two fingers in her throbbing hole as I massaged her clit with my tongue. I began sucking her clit.

"Oh yeah!" She screamed.

"Oh baby."

She released her nectar and I gobbled it up.

"Are you ok?" I rested my head on her stomach.

"Uh huh." She breathed.

"As long as you are pleased." I could feel my dick throbbing.

"But look at you." She pointed to the bulge in my pants.

"Oh yeah. Can I use your bathroom?"

"It's right down the hall."

If I had to jack my dick I would. I wasn't about to have Chante be another one night stand. I thought more of her than that. I made it to her bathroom. It was decorated in purple of course. I pulled out my python and started pulling on it when I heard the door open.

"Oh my!" Chante exclaimed. I guess her ex wasn't working with what I had.

"Do you need a towel or anything?"

"Can you give me a hand?"

She tried to wrap one hand around my pipe but she realized I was long and wide. I was thinking she was wondering how I would feel inside of her.

"Oh Chante." I felt the nut running out.

"You were really backed up." She smiled.

"Yeah, but I will be recharged in thirty minutes."

I looked at the time on my phone, it was 11:35 p.m., and I had seven missed calls. Four of them were from Marcie and the other three were just freaks that I dealt with from time to time.

"Well sweet lady, I guess I'll be leaving now." I grabbed Chante's hand

"Ok Yung." She winked. "What time were you coming by tomorrow?"

"Probably around 4:30 p.m., if that's ok with you." I planted another five minute kiss on her.

"Sounds good."

"Well I will see you later." I kissed her hand and made my way to my ride. I decided to call Marcie back just to see what she wanted. That trick didn't let the phone ring.

"Where have you been?" she yelled.

"Out. What did you want?" I was already pissed.

"I'm sitting in front of your crib!" She hung up the phone.

More drama. I drove to my spot and saw Marcie's green Ford Focus in the driveway. I didn't see her inside the car so Mooch must've let her in.

"Sup Cuz?" Mooch was playing his PS3 in the living room.

"Where is Marcie?"

"She's in the back." He laughed.

I made my way to my room to find Marcie laying across my bed with just her t-shirt and panties on.

"What are you doing?"

"Boy stop playing. You know what I want." She got off the bed and grabbed me by my shirt tail

"I ain't got time for your mess today. Where's the baby?"

"Hmm. Our son is with my momma." She started unfastening my belt and my pants fell to the floor

36

"Stop Marcie!" I wasn't trying go there with this crazy bitch.

"I'm not taking no for an answer." She pulled out my dick and tried to swallow it. I closed my eyes and tried to imagine being inside of Chante. Dayum! Marcie knew how to suck a dick and she swallowed my nut.

"Seems like you missed me."

"Whatever girl." I couldn't let her know how good it was.

"Give me some." Marcie lay on her back.

"Naw, I want you in your ass or not at all." I flipped her over.

She let me but I had to turn my music up loud to drown out her screams. She sucked me off two more times and then I made her go home. I would feel bad but I am a man with needs. I will fuck a bitch. Not Chante though. I'd treat her like a lady.

Chapter Four

Knock Knock Knock.

Damn, I hate being woke up from a good sleep.

"Yung, are you up?" It was a soft and sultry voice.

I yawned, stretched and made my way to the door. It was Renee, an old freak that hung with one of Mooch's freaks.

"Sup." I said sounding uninterested.

"What you been up to? I have been missing you boy." She made her way through my door and to my bed

"Yeah right." I replied.

"I'm for real. I haven't seen you in a few weeks." She licked her thin Asian lips

"Yeah, I been busy." I knew what she missed.

"Can I show you what I missed?"

Before I had time to answer, she pulled out my dick and began to lick it.

"Is that all you missed?" I asked.

But I enjoyed the way she teased me. Renee began to suck harder until I nutted and squirted it on her chest.

"I told you I missed you." She laughed and put me back in her mouth.

"Damn girl!"

I could hear my phone going off. It was Chante. I tried to grab it but the freak made sure I didn't stop what she was doing.

"Fuck that phone." Renee licked on the tip of my dick head. She knew I liked that shit.

"I'm answering this call so be easy." I'd been thinking about Chante all night.

"Hello Yung," Chante replied.

"Hey, what's up?" I moaned as Renee sucked harder

"Were you asleep?"

"Uh huh." I was trying to keep my thoughts together as Renee was massaging my balls.

"Oh, I didn't mean to wake you up. I was just saying hello."

"It's cool. How are you doing?" I breathed into the phone.

"I'm fine." She snickered.

"Yes you are." I bit my lip. I could feel myself about to unload.

"Can I call you back?"

"Sure."

"Ok then."

I hung up the phone just in time. This time I squirted in Renee's face.

"Yung.Why did you do that?" She was pissed

"Because, I wanted to you little freak." I laughed.

She laughed and left my room.

"Yo Cuz." It was Mooch calling me

"Sup bruh?" I yelled.

"Where is Renee?" He looked suspicious.

"She ain't in here. Check the bathroom."

"True. But I'm sure she's been in here." We exchanged dap.

We both laughed. Freaks did serve their purpose, but I wanted something more; something long term. I was getting tired of the fast life. Mooch made his way in the bathroom with Renee as I looked through my closet to find an outfit. It was already 11:00 a.m. Time flies by when you're having fun. I heard my door open and it was Mooch again.

"That freak is off the chain." He winked.

"What did she do?" I asked.

39

"I tried to smash her but she said only if you were down with it." He nodded his head and gave me a wink.

"She wants a threesome?

"Yeah. You down?"

I thought about the fact that I got to get ready to see Chante at 4:30. I also thought about the fact that it might be a while before Chante gives me some booty.

"Yeah, fuck it....let's do it."

***

Four o'clock pm. I was on the way to pick up my future wife. I know I told her 4:30 p.m., but I just can't wait to see her.

Marcie was calling again. I might as well talk to her and get it out of the way.

"Yeah." I replied when I answered the phone. I'm sure she could tell I was aggravated.

"What are you doing?" Marcie said softly.

"I'm chillin'what do you want?"

"Nuthin Boo. Am I gonna get to see you later?"

"I'm busy today and I got some shit to do for my momma." I was getting ready to turn on Chante's street.

"How long is that gonna take?" She whined.

"Bye girl. I will talk to you tomorrow."

"Why?"

I hung up the phone and put it on vibrate. I didn't want any distractions tonight. I checked myself over in my rearview mirror. Dark skinned black man, fresh fade, goatee with the connecting side burns. I checked my outfit and the swag was on point.

I knocked on her door.

"Whassup Yung?" Chante looked like a dream. She was wearing an all-white Baby Phat pantsuit with a pink t-shirt to match. Her hair was pulled into a ponytail and her jewelry and makeup created a perfect picture.

"You. Are you ready to ride for a minute?" I gently kissed her.

"Sure, let me grab my purse and keys." She motioned for me to enter but I stood by the door. I knew if I got too comfortable, my lips would want to explore some more.

"You are a little early." She hurried through the apartment looking for something.

"Yeah. I guess I was just anxious to see you." I licked my lips

"Oh really?" She stood directly in front of me with her hands on her hips. I pulled out my phone. It was only 4:10 p.m. I did have a little time to play.

"Why are you looking at me like that?" I could see her blush.

"Because girl, you're so beautiful." I stood back to really admire her

"Stop it." She grinned and batted her eyes.

I came closer, kissed her gently on the cheek. I ran my hands up and down her arms and eventually wrapped them around her waist. We kissed passionately as she tilted her head back. I gently caressed her breasts and made my way down to her booty... so juicy.

"I want all of you, Chante. Not just some. I have a feeling that you want to be loved just as much as I do." I continued to run my fingers across her belt buckle until I eventually unfastened it. I pulled down her tight pant jeans and white laced panties.

"I want to make you happy. Will you let me? " I blew in her ear while gently rubbing my finger up and down her moist clit.

41

She only moaned. I got down on my knees, parted her legs and sucked each of her pussy lips. I inserted my tongue in her wet hot box like I would with my dick. She was so turned on; she released her juices in my mouth.

"Oh my God." She wailed.

"Yes ma'am. God is good." I kissed her inner thighs and pulled up her panties and pants.

"Yes He is and so are you."

"You just don't know the half."

***

We arrived at my momma's house shortly before 5:00. I could see that April and Shannon's cars were in the carport. I really didn't want to deal with April's mouth but I would try to make it through tonight's dinner.

"Are you ok, Yung?" Chante looked concerned. I guess I still had a fucked up look on my face.

"Oh, I'm cool. My sister, April, is here and we argue a lot." I put on a front and a fake smile.

"Yeah I understand. I have two brothers and they get on my nerves sometimes." She smiled and shook her head.

"Well, you ready?"

"I guess so."

"Alright. Let's go." I took a deep breath.

I was surprised to discover that Chante and my mom had a lot in common. Luckily, Rick, came to dinner. I didn't have to worry about April hating on me with her boo there. I can still see her rolling her eyes at me in disgust.

"So, do you have any kids, Chante?"

All eyes, especially April's, were on Chante.

"Yes ma'am, I have a three year old daughter."

"Well, that's something you have in common with April. Isn't that nice? What's her name?"

"Isis." Chante replied.

"Sounds sweet, you will have to bring her with you the next time you come."

"Hmm." April shook her head.

I immediately stared her down.

"Did you have something to say, April?" Momma loved to put people on blast.

"I was just gonna say..."

"Nuthin, Mrs. DaMone. I'm sure it would be nice for Isis and Ricardo Jr.to play together." Rick said.

"Yes it would." I looked over at April with disgust.

"When are you going to bring your friend back to see me?" Momma was really putting on her charm.

"I'm not sure momma."

"Well, you don't have to be a stranger young lady."

"I'll be sure to come back, ma'am."

"If he is even talking to her for longer than today." April mumbled.

"Excuse me?" Chante motioned at April.

"Look, you seem like you are a really nice chick, so I'm gonna tell you the truth." April cleared her throat.

"Shut up April." My temper began to rise.

"My brother is a hoe."

"April, don't you start this mess today. This young lady is just now meeting us and you are trying to stir up some trouble."

"You better get her momma!" I yelled.

"Everybody calm down." Shannon spoke up. "Chante just ignore my sister. She just likes to have attention."

"Whatever. Y'all know I'm telling the truth." April rolled her eyes.

"Man, we are getting ready to go momma because April is going to make me slap her." I stood up.

"I wish you would." April jumped to her feet. Rick immediately yanked on her arm and made her sit down.

"Well, it was nice meeting you all." Chante looked confused

"Yes dear. Don't you worry about April. Her bark is a lot worse than her bite."

"Whatever." April murmured again.

I hadn't realized I left Chante in the house as I was posted up in my car. She knocked on my door; I'd forget that I had locked it.

"Are you ok?" she asked.

"That bitch makes me sick." I responded. I just wanted to knock her out.

"Come on now. It's not that bad. She is your sister."

"She be on that stupid crap. I hate when people try to be all in my business or try to put lies on me."

"It's ok Yung. You don't have to get so upset."

"I just really wanted things to go smooth tonight." I frowned.

"I enjoyed the dinner minus the April incident." She grabbed my hand.

She looked at me with her lip poked out and we both laughed.

"I want you to be my baby. I don't want anything or anyone to come between what we have." I said, as I pulled the car over at a gas station.

"We will see how things go." She winked.

"Ok, are you going to need a reminder from earlier today?" I licked my lips.

"I don't know. Maybe so."

44

It was 8 p.m., when we made it back to Chante's place. She tried to reassure me that my sister's outburst didn't upset her. I just felt like my business is my business. But I want to build a life with this woman. I don't want anything to get in the way of this blessing.

"Are you going to be uptight for the rest of the night?" Chante motioned closer to me on the sofa. She rubbed on my neck and I tried to relax.

"I'm cool boo. I just don't like stupid shit." I kissed her gently.

"I feel you but let's just enjoy the rest of the night."

She was right though. Why was I over here worrying about unimportant shit? I had the woman I wanted and she was definitely feeling me. I held her in my arms for the rest of the night. We lay in the bed and discussed our past and things we wanted for the future. She said she wanted to feel love and I wanted to be the one to give it to her. I was willing to be done with my bad ways because she was everything and more.

I never wanted to hurt her and I never wanted her to leave me.

Chapter Five

The past couple months had really been intense. I was spending time with Chante every day. She was officially becoming a part of me. I put her and Isis' picture on my phone's screensaver.

"Yo Cuz, so what are we gonna be doing for the 4th of July?"

"Well, we're definitely going by your father's house for some barbecue and then me and Chante have to drop Isis off at her daddy's crib."

"You are really into this chick?" He couldn't believe how serious I was about Chante.

"Yes fam. She means the world to me."

"But, what about the street life?"

"Look Cuz, what I do in the streets, is my business. But just know that Chante is my lady. I will make love to her even though I might hit one of these tricks from time to time." I felt my blood begin to boil.

"My man." Mooch tried to give me dap.

"I'm for real. This is it for me." I reassured him.

We headed to the West Side Barber Shop. I had to stay fly and plus I wanted to celebrate a special occasion tonight. Chante and I had been together for two months now; it was June 26, 2004. I know a lot of cats wouldn't see the point in my celebration but that's the difference between me and the average guy. A woman wants to feel special for no particular reason. It's the little things that seem to mean the most. Shannon helped put me on game. So tonight I think I'm going to make my move and make love to Chante for the very first time. It's been hard holding back, even though I could get them freaks to suck my dick. It was Chante that I always had on my mind.

"Look fam." Mooch was pointing to the familiar green Ford Focus.

"Can I talk to you for a second?" Marcie was headed my way.

"Man, we don't have anything to talk about. The DNA test said Malik was not mine. So you need to go holla at your real baby's daddy. Stop calling me and leave me the hell alone."

I saw the tears welled up in her eyes. My words had stopped her dead in her tracks. She turned and ran back to her car. Moments later, she drove off.

"That was kind of cold, Yung." Mooch lit a cigarette.

"The truth hurts. I'm glad I don't have to deal with her anymore."

I'm glad we made it to the barbershop early on a Friday. It was a little packed but at 9:00 a.m.; we would beat the rush.

"What's happening Yung?" Silas flagged me over. He was a childhood friend and the best barber in town.

"Let me fade you up."

"Yea, you are the only one that I let cut my hair."

"True. I got to keep you looking fly for the ladies." He grinned.

"Naw bruh. He is just focused on one lady nowadays."

"Oh word!" Silas seemed surprised.

"Yea man she's the one."

"Dayum, so you're the one that got Byron's old lady?"

"I guess so." I was a little irritated because I didn't like to think about Chante being anyone else's woman.

"How do you know him?"

"Oh, B cuts hair on the East Side. We speak from time to time but nothing major. I just remember

47

seeing her from time to time but I knew she had left him a while back."

"That's right; a while back and now she's mine for life."

"I hear ya man." Silas chuckled.

"Well she's a good woman from what I hear. B was a fool and wild as hell. Almost as wild as you."

"Don't play yourself Silas. I'm an original. Ain't nobody like me." I was pissed.

My phone rang. It was Chante.

"See what I mean? She be hitting me up first thing in the morning.

"Whassup boo?"

"Hello Yung. I'm fixing Isis some breakfast and waiting on her granny to come get her."

"Oh. Where is my step-daughter going?" I laughed and the dudes in the barbershop looked in amazement.

"She's going over to her granny's. Isis loves it over there because she gets to do whatever she wants. She runs that house."

"I bet she does. Well I'm at the barbershop getting fresh for you. My boy Silas says hello."

"You know him? Tell him I said hello."

"I will baby." I was a little aggravated that another nigga knew my boo, but I had big plans for tonight and I didn't want to lose sight of that.

"I will be over there after I leave the here."

"Oh ok." Chante's phone was going in and out like she was walking around.

"I'm gonna be here. Isis' granny is outside. Talk to you later Babe."

"Later Sweetie."

I felt confident when I hung up the phone. The only thing on my mind was being with Chante and making love to her.

"Cuz, I thought we were going to make some stops today?" Mooch asked.

"Relax. It's early. Just drop me off at my girl's crib and we will meet up again this afternoon."

***

Chante had my nature rising. I was ready to give her the package that I had been carrying. I waited two months; which was the longest I ever went without tagging a chick. I wanted her to feel special and was definitely ready to make my move.

An hour and a half later we pulled up at Chante's apartment complex. I sat in the car with the card and red roses I bought for Chante.

"Dayum Cuz, You went all out for this girl.

"I told you man this chick is special. She's not like the rest of them hoes. She's sweet, smart and about her business. I'm the only thing missing from her life."

"I hear ya man. Hit me up lata."

"Aight, then Cuz."

My hands were full with unexpected gifts. I couldn't wait to see the look on Chante's face. She opened the door as soon as I knocked. She was all smiles when I handed her the card and flowers.

"What's this for?" She said looking at her gifts.

"Two months ago, you walked into my life and I am so thankful." I leaned in for a kiss.

"That's so sweet." she said as she kissed me.

"No boo, you're sweet."

Chante walked into the kitchen to find something to put the roses in. When she returned, she had them

49

in a pretty purple vase and put them on the living room table.

"I'm glad you like them. I've never bought flowers for a woman before." I grabbed her hand and brought her closer to me.

"I find that hard to believe. You seem so smooth."

"It's you. You make me want to be a better man." I held her face in my hands.

We held our glance as she led me into her bedroom. The lights were dim and the radio was playing slow jams. I picked her up and she wrapped her legs around my waist and I swayed from side to side. Her tongue felt juicy as she slid it in and out of my mouth.

"Are you ready for all of me?" I whispered in her ear.

"Yes, I want to feel you."

I laid her back on the bed. I began removing my clothes and I removed hers as well. We tongue wrestled while I lay on top of her. I gently caressed her body as I had so many times before.

"Let me feel you Yung." She whimpered.

"That's all you had to say."

My dick was throbbing. I hoped I didn't bust early.

"Do you have protection?" she asked.

"I got a Magnum in my pocket. Are you on the pill?"

"Yes." She breathed.

"Well, do I need the condom? I wanna feel you. Please."

"Are you sleeping with anyone else?"

"No. I have been saving myself for you." I lied.

"Well, you have been patient. Just don't hurt me," She was caving in.

"I promise I won't babe."

She opened her legs and I stuck the head of my dick inside her.

"Oh my!"

"That's just the head baby." I said confidently.

"Dayum baby. I don't know if I can handle the rest."

I managed to get all eight inches inside her hot and wet pussy. Dayum, she had a good grip on my dick. Every stroke felt like a piece of heaven. I had to pull out and kiss that cat just to avoid an early nut.

"Baby I breathed as the sweat poured down my face.

"I wanna cum inside of you...can I...can I...oh shit."

I felt my body quiver with delight and my heart was pounding. I lay on top of my queen, breathing heavily and kissing her softly on her cheek.

"That was really something. Wow." She whispered.

"You are really something babe."

"Yeah and your phone is about to vibrate off of the table."

She headed to the bathroom to freshen up. I looked at my phone six missed calls and three text messages. The texts were from Marcie saying she really needed to talk to me. Bullshit, cuz had called three times and the other three calls were from freaks. I decided to give Mooch a call.

"What's up Cuz? You must have been in the zone over there."

"Mind your business. What's up?"

"We need to make these moves, you feel me? When are you going to be ready?"

"Dayum! Can it wait or do we have to do it now?" I patted my head. It was only 12:30 and I didn't want to leave my girl this soon

51

"Come on man. You know time is money."

"I hear ya. Give me about thirty minutes and come on."

"Alright ready."

I didn't want to leave but I needed to make this run to cover me for the next month or two. Ten thousand dollars apiece for me and Mooch. After that we could chill for a minute if we wanted too.

"So you have to go?" She pouted.

"Yes boo, but I'm gonna call you a little later."

"Oh yeah. I guess I will try to find something to do until then."

"That's whassup. You wanna come by my house and chill?"

"We can." She smiled.

"I will call you as soon as I get finished. My cousin is going out of town for the weekend and I will have the pad all to myself."

I winked at my baby. Again my phone was buzzing. This time it was Marcie. I sent her to voicemail.

"You are a busy man." Chante had her eyes on my phone.

"But I am never too busy for you." I winked.

"Maybe one day you can tell me what it is that you do." She raised her eyebrow.

"Yeah. We can talk about it later."

My phone was vibrating again. This time it was Mooch.

"I'm outside." He hung up.

I gave her a hug. "Well boo, that was my cousin. I will see you later."

"Ok. I will see you later." She said then kissed me.

"Well you can call me in a few and I will try to get finished as soon as possible."

"You better." She chuckled.

"I will boo." I headed to Mooch's car.

***

Chante stayed in the back of my mind but now it was time to get to the money. Mooch and I had a great connect on that loud in Ohio. We would make runs and get paid a grip for our trouble. We headed to the PJ's to meet with Big Earl.

"What time did dude say to be here?"

I was getting anxious. I wanted to get this shit out of the way because I had other things to do. Around about that time, we saw the grey Phantom with tinted windows, pull up. Big boy status. Big Earl had his hands in all the illegal trades in the state. Dude had politicians and police in his back pockets. The Feds hated him because they could never find actual evidence on him. Earl was always three steps ahead of the law. He made me nervous because I used to fuck his daughter on the regular before she went away to college at Chapel Hill last fall. She still stays in touch but Earl would probably try to kill me if he knew I turned his daughter out.

"What's the deal fellas?" He asked and motioned us over to his car.

"Chillin'." Mooch nodded.

"Let's ride. Glad to see you fellas, y'all are my most trusted Superstars."

"Word. I love getting that bread. It's easy money."

"True. How long do you think it will take for you to make the drop?" Earl asked as he smoked his Cuban cigar.

Mooch scratched his head.

"Round trip? Or just making it up there?" I asked.

"Just making it up there." Earl stared at me in his rearview mirror.

53

"That's about a ten hour drive," I said with confidence because we had made that trip at least three times before.

"Ok, I'm gonna change things up a little bit. Since I know I can trust you two, I'm going to give you guys $5,000 a piece right now. Of course, you will get the other $5,000 when you get back." Earl pulled over at a local restaurant

"Thanks man." Mooch was excited.

"Yeah thanks." I replied.

"Thank y'all for being trustworthy for all these years. Y'all stay out of trouble and always come through when I need y'all. You know the holiday is coming up, so to avoid some heat, we need to do this before the fourth of July.4th. The thirtieth of June is Monday, so make the move then."

"No problem." I felt good. I would be able to chill with Chante for the weekend without any distractions but she might wonder where I was the following week.

"Yeah that's cool." Mooch agreed.

"I gotta holla at my baby's mom this weekend anyway."

"So it's settled. I'll give y'all a call on Sunday and we will conduct our business on Monday. Here's some of the money. Don't spend it all on one chick."

We all laughed.

"Yung just might do that." Mooch joked.

"You got a winner?" Earl smiled.

"Yes sir." I nodded.

"That's good." Earl looked surprised because he always thought of me as a playboy.

"Hold on to her. Don't let any sideline ass get in the way."

"I'm already on it." I nodded in agreement.

54

We made our way back to our crib. Mooch was talking about going to the mall and getting some new jewelry.

"Dude, you got more chains than these hood rats around here."

"Don't worry about it. You got your way to ball and I have mine." He seemed a little offended

"True." I mumbled under my breath.

"But right now I'm thinking about calling some freaks. Let's see what they will do for some change."

"Anything!" I hollered.

"What about Jennifer and Renee?" Mooch went through his phone.

"Naw cuz. We already had that episode." I replied.

"What about Jess and Rebecca?" He winked.

Jess and Rebecca were two hot, rich, white college chicks. They were living off of their daddy's money. They loved riding around in BMWs and they loved to come to the PJs and getting some of this black dick.

"Yeah, call them up. We can keep our money. Hell, they might pay us."

"I feel you bruh." Mooch made the call and the freaks said they would be over in a little while.

My phone rang. And it was Chante.

"Hey baby." I smiled.

"Hey back at cha. Are you still busy?"

"Yeah." A little bit but I'm going to be finished in about an hour or two. Were you missing me?"

"A little." She chuckled.

"Oh." I saw Jess' BMW pulling up.

"That's what I wanted to hear."

"Uh huh." She replied.

"Well, I'm going to call you when I get finished, ok Babe?"

"Ok. Talk to you later." She sounded disappointed.

"Later Babe."

In come the freaks. Two blond hair and blue eyed party girls, in a hurry to get on this dick.

"Whassup Yung?" Jess headed in my direction. Her pink tank top was a size too small for those grapefruits she was carrying.

"How have you been Jess? What do you have for me today?"

"What about me? She was a knockout, but dumb blonds aren't my thing.

"Don't worry baby daddy is here for you." Mooch picked her up.

"Take me away daddy!"

Mooch threw her over his shoulder like a bag of potatoes and headed to his bedroom.

"So whassup?" I put my hand on my dick. I saw her eyes following my hand movements. I pulled out my dick and started stroking it in front of her.

"That's whassup." Jess made her move to the couch. She sat on top of me in the backward cowgirl position.

"Put it in my ass daddy."

"Shit." I loved fucking these hoes in their asses because it was probably cleaner than their ran-through pussy.

"You want it, you put it in there. She mounted her ass directly on my python.

"Oh yeah daddy."

"What did you say little freak?" I liked to talk dirty to them because it turned them on.

"Oh yeah, daddy." Jess bounced her flat booty up and down on my dick, riding me and rubbing on my nuts.

"You gonna let me cum in your face this time?" I bounced her up and down harder as her head and titties rocked from side to side.

"Answer me girl."

"Oh yes daddy!" She screamed.

I felt myself almost ready to let go. I didn't worry about lasting a longtime with these freaks. Hell, I was just trying to get a nut off.

"OK, get up and catch this nut."

She rose up and stroked my dick until I came in her face. The freaky bitch rubbed it in and licked her fingers.

"Damn girl." I said and wiped the sweat from my forehead.

"Yung.Why don't you ever eat me or hit me in my pussy?"

"Why do you have to ask so many damn questions? Did you climax?"

"Hell yeah!"

"Did it feel good?"

"Yes." She licked her lips.

"So why are you complaining?"

"I was just asking?" She seemed so clueless.

"I got a woman. She gets the special treatments, ok?" I was honest, even if she didn't like what I had to say.

"Why don't you go back there with my cousin...he might eat you."

She stormed off and made her way to Mooch's room. He might eat off of those hoes, but I won't. It takes a special lady to get this tongue. I don't love those hoes. I didn't have to fuck her at all. She ought to be happy with what she got.

"Hey cuz! Y'all need to wrap it up back there because my girl is coming over here. So everybody needs to get the fuck out." I hollered.

I tried my best to keep my street life away from my boo because too much of the truth would only hurt her. I didn't want to hurt her.

***

By 6:00 the house was cleared out. I did my best vacuuming and cleaning up. I didn't want any evidence of hoes being there. Chante really meant a lot to me and I didn't want to lose her because of the street life.

The sound of my phone ringing broke me out of my thoughts. It was Marcie. I had no idea why this bitch was still calling me?

"What do you want?" I hollered.

"Look, I know I hurt you and I'm sorry but I still have feelings for you." She sobbed.

"I'm not hurt so I don't see why you are still calling me." I corrected

"I don't want to lose you in my life." She cried.

"Look Marcie, I'm not mad at you. I wish you all the best. But I got to go. Me and my girl are hanging out."

"Girl? What girl?" She screamed.

"None of your business!"

"She's coming over to your house? We will see about that."

She hung up. I put the phone on vibrate. I'm glad I decided to drive over to Chante's house. We could ride back in her car because none of the freaks knew her car. I just hope Marcie didn't start any of her usual bullshit.

I headed to Chante's and was sending Marcie's calls to voicemail. I thought about getting my number changed but I had too many contacts for that bullshit. Maybe the girl will just move on and find someone else to bother.

"What up babe?" I kissed Chante as I made my way in her crib.

"Hey, I thought you wanted to chill at your house?"

"I do baby. But I'm trying to avoid anyone from stopping by. So, can we ride over there in your car?"

"I guess so. Who do you think will come by?" Chante looked a little suspicious.

"No one important, but I just want you all to myself."

My phone continued to vibrate as we made our way back to my spot. I guess Chante noticed how annoyed I had become.

"What's the problem?" She looked concerned.

"It's nothing babe." I lied.

"It doesn't seem like nothing. Why don't you just answer your phone?"

"Because I don't want to "to"

I continued to send Marcie's call to voicemail, but it didn't seem to stop her from calling.

"It's a girl from my past. The one that was trying to pin her baby on me."

"Oh really? I thought you said it wasn't your baby?" She looked pissed.

"It's not." I said with confidence.

"So why is she still calling?"

"I don't know babe."

"Well let me talk to her the next time she calls." Chante was really upset.

"I doubt that will do any good." I felt my phone buzzing and handed her the phone.

59

"Hello." Chante said calmly as she put the call on speakerphone.

"Who the fuck is this?" Marcie yelled.

"This is Yung's woman and why do you keep calling him?"

"Bitch, I will do what I want."

"I got your bitch! Call all you want but I guarantee he won't answer, dumb bitch."

Chante hung up the phone.

"I told you the girl was crazy." I leaned over and kissed my lady.

"I see, but sometimes hearing another woman's voice will make her think twice about calling." Chante laughed it off.

"Or maybe not." I held up my phone and saw that Marcie was calling again.

"What do you want?" Chante asked.

I could hear Marcie screaming and probably hating on me but Chante never showed any emotion.

"Well whatever little girl...I'm cutting the phone off, so have fun with that."

Chante cut off my phone and we both laughed as we entered my crib.

"Looks like you keep your place nice and clean. I have never seen a bachelor's pad so organized."

"Yeah, I wanted everything to look nice for you babe," I grinned.

"So how many other chicks do I have to worry about calling or stopping by?"

"You don't have to worry baby. You are the only woman that I want and need."

Chante had me thinking. Marcie could decide to drive by at any time. I dimmed all the lights and we made our way to my bedroom. With my phone off, I didn't have to worry about the calls but I didn't want anyone to stop by. Chante seemed a little skeptical about the way I was acting but I tried my best to seem happy. The truth was I didn't want anyone or anything to ruin the romance that we had started. I'd never felt this way about any other female and I didn't want it to end because of some stupid hoe. I'd be lying if I said that I didn't sleep with one eye open that night. Luckily no drama.

Chapter Six

I woke up Saturday to the smell of bacon, eggs and pancakes from the kitchen. I guess my baby did some grocery shopping while I was asleep. I wondered what time it was but remembered that my phone had been cut off from the night before.

"Good morning sleepyhead. She met me in the hall before I made it to the bathroom and hugged me.

'Good morning love." I said kissing her forehead.

"It really smells good in the kitchen."

"I did the best I could. Get cleaned up and join me." She smiled.

"I will babe."

I went to the bathroom stopped to get my phone first. I had to check my phone. I immediately noticed my voicemail was full. I had thirty text messages and fifty missed calls. Most of them were from Marcie but my mom, sister and cousin had been calling too. It was 10:30 a.m. I figured I might as well call my mom.

"Good morning Momma." I smiled as I made my way to the kitchen.

"Don't hello me." Momma was pissed.

"I called you last night and this morning. What's going on?"

"Nothing Ma. Marcie kept calling, so I cut my phone off last night."

"I never liked that girl. I thought she would have left you alone since she found out that baby wasn't yours."

"Yea, I hope she finds her baby daddy and leaves me alone."

"She knows who it is." Momma sounded serious.

"Oh really? So why is she buggin' me?"

"Because it is Chante's ex, Byron."

"What?" I hollered. The sound of my voice startled Chante.

"What's wrong Yung?" She seemed concerned.

"Nothing babe." I lied because I didn't want to be the one to tell her the news.

"So Chante doesn't know?" Momma asked.

"No." I said.

"Well, you need to tell her."

"That's not my place." Chante raised an eyebrow.

"Let me talk to her."

"No Momma."

"Look boy," Momma hollered.

"I was trying to tell you about this yesterday. I know how to be calm when I talk to people. Everyone in the neighborhood knows anyway because you know Marcie has a big mouth. She actually thinks this ordeal is funny. She's been telling people that Chante will have to deal with her since they have kids by the same guy."

"I hear you Ma. We will just come over there after breakfast, ok?" My blood was beginning to boil.

"Ok son. Tell Chante I said hello."

"I will Ma."

I tried to remain calm as I sat my phone down.

"Is everything ok?" Chante looked worried.

"No, not really but let's eat and then we can go by my mom"

"What's wrong?" Chante began to look nervous.

"We'll talk about it over there."

"Yung ,I told you that I don't like surprises, so just tell me." She pushed her plate away from her

"My mom wants to talk to you."

"Is it something bad?"

"I promise baby, everything is going to be ok. Go on and take a shower. We can go when you are dressed,"

"I don't like the sound of this." She arose from the table and made her way to the bathroom. I waited until I heard her lock the bathroom door. When she turned the water on, I attempted to call Marcie.

"Look bitch, I don't know what kind of game you are trying to play but it ends here. You stay the hell away from me and my girl."

"Don't you threaten me Victor; I'll have to deal with her regardless because we have the same baby daddy. I didn't know that was the chick you were dating. I tried to tell you about it the other day but you wouldn't talk to me."

"Well, I know now, so just stop calling and texting me. Call him." I cut her off.

"I got his number, but you are the one that I want." She chuckled.

"You can't have me, bitch."

"We'll see about that."

"What's that supposed to mean?" I said.

"We will see if that chick still wants you after I have a real talk with her."

I made my way to the front door. "Bitch, if you ever try to cross me, I will make your life a living hell."

"Oh yeah?" She yelled.

"You know what I am capable of, so don't play dumb."

"Well, I just wanted a little of your time. Think about that or kiss your perfect little woman goodbye."

Marcie hung up. I couldn't believe this bitch was actually trying to blackmail me. I had to think fast.

Marcie didn't know everything about me but she knew enough to cause some problems.

"Are you ready?" Chante made her way to the door.

"Yea, I'm ready." I sighed and locked the front door. We headed to the car.

"Did you want to get your truck from my house?"

"Yeah, I guess we can do that."

I just couldn't get past the comment Marcie had made to me earlier. This bitch was taking things too far.

"Yung!" Chante shouted.

"Yes babe." I snapped out of my thoughts.

"You just passed your mom's house. Are you ok?"

"Oh yeah. My bad baby."

"You are really making me nervous with the way you are acting,"

"I'm sorry boo."

I only hoped Chante wouldn't end up hating me after she talked to my mom. The only reason Marcie told everyone about the situation was to get back at me. She was just trying to make Chante's life hard because we were together.

"Whassup bruh? I been trying to call you." Shannon smiled.

"Yeah, I talked to momma this morning. That's why we are over here."

"Well, I guess I can stick around. Why don't you go on inside, Chante. My mom is waiting on you."

"What? What's this all about?" Chante really looked confused

Her phone began to ring but Chante didn't seem interested in whoever was calling.

"What do you want?" Chanted rolled her eyes.

"I need to talk to you Cha." It was Byron.

"I'm busy right now Byron, so it's gonna have to wait."

"Talk to him babe." I whispered.

"What? Would someone please tell me what the hell is going on?"

"I got another baby, Cha." Byron blurted out.

"Well congrats B." Chante tried to sound interested.

"Don't act like you don't care." He responded.

"Why should I? We're not together!"

"I know that." He paused.

"It was a one night stand. I didn't know the baby was mine until a week ago. It's a three month old boy."

"Well, you finally have the son that you always wanted."

"That's not all." He paused.

"What else is there to say?"

"I got a baby by this crazy bitch named Marcie. She used to mess with your boy, Yung."

"What the fuck?"

"Yeah, I'm sorry Cha. She means nothing to me but apparently she wanted to have a baby by Yung."

"I got to go Byron." Chante hung up the phone. I could see the tears welling up in her eyes.

"Are you ok baby?" I motioned over in her direction.

"Don't call me that. Shannon could you please drive me home?" She was obviously hurt.

"I can drive you." I was offended.

"Bruh let me speak to you for a minute." Shannon jumped in.

"I'll be waiting by your car." Chante ran to Shannon's car as she wiped the tears from her eyes.

"What's all that about?" I looked over at Shannon.

"She has every reason to be embarrassed and hurt." Shannon was always the voice of reason. "Chante just found out her ex has a baby by someone her current boyfriend was dating."

"I see your point. But why is she mad at me?"

"She is just hurt. I will take her home and I will let you know what's up."

"I just don't want to lose her. I told Marcie to back off."

"When did you talk to Marcie?"

"This morning after I talked to momma. She said if I didn't want to lose Chante, I better spend some time with her."

"Bruh, Stop talking to her, period. I'll handle her. Wait until I see her stupid ass."

"Don't get into any trouble." I cautioned her.

"Oh you know I'm good. But for now, let me take your girl home and we can talk when I get back." Shannon popped her collar.

"Thanks sis. I don't know what I would do without you"

"Yeah, yeah. I'm just gonna charge that to your bill." She smiled.

I stood at the front door as Shannon and Chante pulled out of the driveway. They appeared to be talking but Chante would look not in my direction. I wondered what she was thinking but I knew my sister would let me know everything when she got back.

"Who is that at the door?" April asked

"It's just me." I closed the door behind me.

"Well I guess you know that Marcie is going around running her mouth." She snapped her neck.

"Yeah and I'm sure you think it's funny."

"Naw, I think it's sad. I don't feel sorry for you, but I do feel sorry for your girl. You should have left her alone and let her live her life. But no, you always got to be the man."

"I don't have time for this right now April."

"Look bruh, I know we always fight but I just want you to hear me out. Either end things with Chante or do right by her. Don't be like daddy was to momma."

April hugged me and left the house. I never really thought of myself as a reflection of my father. But since she brought it up, maybe I was acting like him. Maybe April was finally right about something for once in her life. I tried to call Chante but she wouldn't answer her phone. I tried to call Shannon's phone next.

"Hey bruh," Shannon said dryly.

"What's going on over there? I been trying to call Chante and she won't answer the phone."

"Calm down bruh. I'm over here with her. I should be on my way in about thirty minutes, ok?"

"But what's going on? Do I need to come over there?"

"No bruh, I will be over there to talk to you," She said strongly.

"Ok, well hurry up."

"Aiight."

Shannon hung up, but I was still so unsure. I could tell when my sister was holding things from me. I really wanted to just ride over there. But Shannon told me not to, so I was trying to occupy my time until she got back.

"What are you doing, son? Where Chante?" Momma made her way down the stairs.

"Shannon took her home."

"Took her home?" Momma looked out the window and noticed Shannon's car was missing. "And why did she do that?"

"She found out about Byron and Marcie." I hung my head.

"You told her," Momma patted me on my back.

"No, Byron called and told her." I looked down in disgust

Momma wrapped her arms around me. "Well, it was bound to come out because the truth always does. Are you ok?"

"I guess Ma. I just hope this doesn't cause us to have problems. I really care about Chante."

"I can see that sweetie."

"Marcie is playing games with my future. She better stop messin' with me."

"Calm down Victor, You just have to give Chante a little time. This is a lot for anyone to digest at one time. Think about it from her point of view. The man she has a daughter with now has a son by a female that is obviously infatuated with her current boyfriend."

"I know momma." I sat down at the kitchen table and lit one of my momma's cigarettes.

"I don't know how I would feel if that happened to me. Her past is clashing with her present life."

"I just don't want to lose her. I don't want to lose her because some trick couldn't keep her legs closed."

"But baby, you were with Marcie just like that other guy. If Chante can't accept all of this, you can't just blame Marcie."

"You're not helping momma." Shannon chimed in. "Stop talking like that. She and bruh will be ok."

I ran over and hugged my sister. I knew she had talked to Chante for me.

"Since when have you been the expert in relationships? You're still a baby yourself."

Shannon and I made our way to the garage. We know momma would only try to see the negative side of the situation. She felt like love was dead because of the way our father treated her. We tried to tell her that she needed to see a therapist.

"So talk to me. What happened when you took my boo home?"

"Come on in the car bruh." Shannon made her way to her vehicle and unlocked the passenger side door. She opened her ashtray and handed me the nicely rolled Swisher.

"It's like that?" I was really getting nervous.

At that moment my phone began to ring, I looked and it was Chante.

"Hello." My sister looked at me as I took a pull from the swisher.

"Hi Yung." Chante's voice sounded so soft.

"Whassup baby? Are you ok?"

"No,'m not ok. This shit that's going on is not ok." She cried.

"I know baby. I'm sorry for all the pain that you are going through."

"Anyways, I just called to tell you that I'm not mad at you. I'm glad you told me about your situation with Marcie from the very beginning. I knew you had messed with her because you told me. You was real about that and I can respect you for that. Byron never mentioned it. I'm not mad that he has another baby because we are through. But I hate that my daughter has a brother by a crazy bitch that wants my man."

"That's right baby, I am your man." I smiled.

Shannon smiled. She knew that things were going to be ok. She didn't have to give me a pep talk. The magic was still there between us. Marcie was not able to break the bond that we shared.

"You are my man." She sniffled.

"Can your man come and see his baby?"

"Yes baby. Please come over here."

Chapter Seven

I would love to say that things were great once Chante and I decided to stay together, but that would be a lie. I had to stop riding with Chante to drop off Isis at her dad's crib. For some reason, Marcie always seemed to be there. I guess there's no end to what some hoes will try to do because a man doesn't want them. Chante knew that I loved her but I also knew how Marcie's bull got on her nerves. Today was just one of those days.

I had practically moved into her crib. Six months into a relationship with this girl, and honestly I couldn't imagine not waking up beside her.

The phone rang and it was Chante on the line.

"Whassup babe?"

"Uggh, that damn girl is getting on my nerves."

"What happened?"

"She was over Ms. Cassie's talking about her son needs this and her son needs that. I mean, Byron told me that he pays $650 a month in child support and she still wants more."

"Yeah, that's Marcie."

"I could tell Ms. Cassie was ready for her to leave because she kept making up things she had to do just to get the girl out of her house."

"That's too bad babe. Where was Byron during all of that?"

"He finally showed up. Isis was mad because she wanted some alone time with her daddy. Marcie and I had words because she tried to say that I'm teaching my daughter to hate her son."

"What?"

"Yea, Byron took her outside, probably gave her greedy ass some money and then she left."

"Better him than me."

"Oh yeah, but unfortunately I still have to deal with her ass."

"I hate that, babe."

"Yeah and now I have to worry about Malik's 1st birthday party. Of course Ms. Cassie is going all out with the party decorations because she is like that with all her grandkids."

"How many does she have?"

"Five in all. Byron has two. Her daughter, Bianca, has a daughter. And her youngest son, Bradley, has two children."

"And she spoils them all?"

"Yes babe," She chuckled.

"Those kids are her world. Mr. Williams just goes along with the program. He knows better than to tell Ms. Cassie that she can't spoil their grandkids."

"You are my world, babe." I smiled.

"Aww baby, are you at home?"

"Yes boo, but I'm getting ready to make some moves with Mooch."

"Oh, I was gonna cook when I got home." She whined.

"That's cool babe. I shouldn't be gone all night. What are you cooking?"

"I guess you will find out when you get home."

"Ok babe." I hated to miss her meals. Everyone says I'm getting fat but my baby kept me full.

"Is Mooch stopping by for dinner? I just wanted to have enough food for everyone."

"He might, but you can cook enough for just us." I didn't like sharing my food with niggas.

"Alright boo. I will see you later."

"Later boo."

I made my way to Mooch's spot. It was still the jump-off spot, but not on a regular because I'm staying with Chante now. Mooch's brother, Marco, moved into the pad. He's twenty but has a lot of heart. Marco always looked up to us and loves the opportunity to hang with the big dawgs. I pulled up in front of Mooch's spot and saw Marco talking to a car load of females. Probably some loose chicken heads that noticed his BMW sitting on chrome eighteens.

"What's happening family?" Marco smiled as he continued to post up on the red Volvo filled with chicks.

"I see you are the man. Hello ladies." I gave them a sly grin as I made my way to the front door.

"Dayum, who is that?" one of the chicks hollered

"Oh, that's my big cuz, Yung." Marco replied.

"Nice to meet you ladies." I smiled and entered the apartment.

I didn't have time to fuck with those females, this was about some business. Mooch was sitting in the living room playing his PS3.

"Whassup Bruh?" Mooch's face never left the screen. He was probably playing Madden.

"You wanted to see me, remember?" I hated it when Mooch tried to play dumb.

"Yeah, let me save this game first."

"Ok. You got any beers in the fridge?" I headed to the kitchen

"Yeah man, help yourself. I'm about to join you." Mooch got up from the couch to cut off the game

I opened the fridge and helped myself to one of the ice cold Bud Lights. Mooch soon joined me and cracked open a can.

"So whassup?" I asked.

"Man, I had to talk to you in person about this shit."

"What's wrong Cuz?" I was becoming concerned.

"It's been a lot of talk on the east side about Chante, Byron and Marcie's mess."

"What do you mean?" I was getting upset.

"You know Snake?" Mooch took another gulp of his beer while I tried to remember that name. "From Boxer Lane? His baby brother Marcus hangs with Marco?"

"Oh, he has twins by big booty Cherrie from the west side?"

"Yeah." Mooch smiled.

"Yeah, I remember when we tag teamed her ass a couple years ago."

Mooch gave me some dap. "I'm still hitting her every now and then."

"Dayum cuz, but what about Snake?" I laughed.

"He said he was buying some CDs at the East Side Barbershop and he overheard Byron talking."

"Oh yeah, what was he talking about?" I said raising my eyebrow

"Snake said he was talking about how he never should have let Chante go and she was the only woman that he ever loved. He said he wanted to be with her but he doesn't know how to get her back because of Marcie and his son. Snake also said Marcie should be with you and he should be with Chante."

"Fuck that nigga. We can go by his shop right now." I was heated

"Hold on cuz, we don't need the heat right now. We probably got another move to make. If you go over there, you know what's going to happen."

"Damn. You're right." I swung my fists in the air

"Don't worry. We'll catch up to him." he said trying to calm me down

75

"Thanks for putting me up on game though." I gave him a handshake and helped myself to another beer. I felt the jealousy building up in my stomach. I just wanted to check on my baby and see what's up with her. I called and she answered on the first ring.

"Hello Babe." Chante sounded joyful.

"Hey Babe. What are you doing?"

"Just finishing up your dinner,"

"Oh. Have you talked to Byron?"

"Not lately. Why would you ask me about that clown?" She seemed shocked.

"Word on the street is that he wants you back because Marcie wants me."

"What? Are you serious? Who told you that?" She laughed.

"It really doesn't matter who said it. I was just letting you know what was going on."

"Well, I don't want him. I'm happy with you. So don't worry about what anyone else says."

"Ok babe I won't." I lied.

"I love you."

"I love you too See you later." I was still pissed.

I hung up the phone. I felt like Chante loved me but I knew how niggas were. Byron was really starting to piss me off. And as soon as I got the chance to confront him, I would.

***

"I'm telling you cuz, we need to hit the club up tonight."

"Naw, I'm cool. I'm chilling with my lady." I laughed. After about six or seven beers, I was feeling a nice buzz.

"Awe, come on Yung. You never wanna hang out anymore. Whassup with that? Can the homeboys get a night with you?"

"Chill out Marco I'm not worried about them hoes. I got the woman I want."

"Yeah man, but a freak every now and then won't hurt you."

We all laughed. I looked at my phone. It was only 4:30. Maybe we could ride out to a couple of stops but I planned on being home with Chante tonight. But since I'm out, I can chill for a little while.

"Why don't we ride by Buckhead Park? Isn't Craig and them supposed to be barbecuing today?"

"Yeah free food, free beer, card games, dominoes, music and the honeys."

"Whose car are we ridin' in?"

"Let's ride in the BMW. I'm driving because you are already drunk."

"Let's go." Marco handed me the keys. Each of us took turns using the bathroom, checking our swag and then headed to the car.

Buck head Park was well known for the freaks and was conveniently next to the West Side Liquor Store. It's been in the neighborhood for years. I can remember having my first kiss and first blowjob by the swing set. Those were the days; back in middle school and high school.

It appeared to be a nice crowd already forming in the park. I parked next to Craig's grey Lincoln Navigator. Craig Benson was a neighborhood friend from way back and he had recently won the lottery. I think he hit for four or five million. Some guys have all the luck. But Craig really needed it. He had lost his job, his house was in foreclosure and his wife was threatening to leave him. The right combination of numbers got his family back on the straight and narrow. Like I said, Craig needed it. With a wife and three demanding daughters; it will cost a lot of money to keep them happy. And I believe his wife is now pregnant with a baby boy.

"Dayum. Look at all these hoes." Marco said stumbling out of the car.

"Chill out bruh. Don't start acting crazy. We just got here," Mooch said hitting Marco in his side.

"I'm ok."

"I bet I get more numbers than you." He put on his sunglasses and straightened his hat.

"How much?"

"Thirty bucks." Marco pulled his money out of his wallet. Marco carried tens, twenties, fifties and hundred dollar bills because the boy loved to floss. We had   cut him into some of our runs. Ten thousand dollars a month was starting to get to his head.

"Ok. But fifty dollars says I hit most of the chicks whose numbers I'm getting today."

"Oh it's on." Marco pulled out a fifty dollar bill. At that moment, two redbones walked by the BMW.

"Hello ladies." I gave them my sly grin.

"Hi cutie." The one in the green and blue sundress replied. I simply nodded my head.

"You ladies aren't leaving are you?" Marco said.

"I was thinking about it." The other redbone replied.

"You should definitely stay, walk back with us and keep us company." Mooch made his way in between the two ladies.

"Yes." Marco smiled showing his deep dimples that complimented his grey eyes.

"And what do you think cutie?" Redbone in the green and blue looked at me.

"Oh don't worry about him. He is taken, but me and my brother are available."

78

"Sorry ma'am." I smiled.

"Come on ladies. Let's get a plate and a nice sitting bench." Marco said placing himself next to the other redbone.

The four of them walked a little ahead of me which was cool. I got tired of hearing my cousins run the same dead end lines on these girls. It's always about how much money they have and if the chick acts right; she might get this or that. They are basically buying the pussy. In my philosophy, the chicks are buying my dick. It's way more women in the world, so we men have more options. So why pay for the coochie? But I must admit, I enjoy watching these niggas ran their game.

We managed to find a nice red picnic table under a tree. It had a traditional red and white checkered table cloth with a barbecue grill nearby. Craig went all out. There was good food and good music was playing.

We had learned that the girls' names were Danielle and Stephanie.

"So, Danielle what are you doing after the barbecue?" Mooch had his arm around the redbone in the pink and silver.

"That depends. "What would you like for me to be doing, Big Baller?" she said wiping sauce from the corner of Mooch's mouth.

"If you act right, you could be doing me."

"Oh really?" She winked at him.

"What about you, Ms. Stephanie?" Marco looked at baby girl in the blue and green.

"I guess we can hangout for a little while." She slyly glanced over at me. I only smiled and continued to eat my ribs.

"What time were y'all heading out?" I looked over at Marco, who was now whispering in Stephanie's ear.

"It's whenever cuz."

"Y'all ready now?" I looked at my phone and noticed it was only five thirty.

"Yeah man. I gotta get my new boo something sexy from Victoria's Secret and I'ma get her nails done too." Marco said getting up from the picnic bench.

"Dayum cuz." I shook my head. Marco was just trying to look better than his brother.

"Yeah bruh, I'm down for that. Let's ride to the mall." Mooch spoke up.

Both girls were all smiles.

"Ladies, why don't y'all follow us to my cousin's crib and then y'all can all ride together."

"You don't want to pick out something for your girl?" Marco said slyly.

"My baby knows that she can get whatever she wants and right now, she has dinner waiting on me." I stared him down.

"Ok." Mooch replied. He knew that I didn't like any man asking questions that involved Chante.

"So they can follow us and you can get home."

"That's whassup." I said.

I got in the driver's seat and exited the park. I never said a word because I was pissed. Mooch and Marco kept discussing their plans with their new found chicks. I could care less. I wasn't interested in a cheap thrill. I had the real thing and I couldn't wait to get home.

Chapter Eight

Life was good. My boo and I had been together almost a year. It had been crazy dealing with Marcie and her bullshit but overall we were happy. Chante had been a nervous wreck lately because Ms. Cassie wanted her to help plan Malik's first birthday party. Why not have Marcie plan it? But thinking about it, Marcie didn't plan to have Malik, so she might not know what she to do. It burned her up to know that Chante and I were still going strong.

Unfortunately Byron had fallen into her trap. A couple months back he decided it was cheaper to keep her. He moved Marcie and Malik into his crib. That ended the child support but it didn't stop Marcie from wanting money. She wanted her hair done, new outfits, new car (a 2009 Chevy Impala), and spending money. That girl could suck a mean one but there's no way I could cake her. I'm sure Byron did his dirt on the side because Marcie would do hers. She had been was pregnant by him again but she miscarried. That slut had really been milking Byron since then; blaming stress as the cause of her miscarriage. Now he feels sorry for encouraging her to work and he feel like he owes her something because she lost their baby. Dumb nigga, she'd been fucking other dudes, it could have been another man's baby.

"Yes Ms. Cassie." Chante was up early on this Saturday morning.

"I got the Spiderman plates, cups and balloons. Uh huh, ok. See you around ten- thirty"

Chante was getting herself and Isis ready to go over to Ms. Cassie's to help with the Malik's birthday party.

"Good morning Yung." Isis smiled while standing in the bedroom doorway.

"Good morning, princess. Where's my hug?"

"I thought you wouldn't ask" she said smiling.

I lifted her up and she hugged my neck. It was our morning ritual. Isis was four going on five; I had been in her life for almost a year now. I couldn't help but to want another baby in the picture though. I think I'm gonna talk to Chante about it.

"Isis Lashay!" Chante hollered as she made her way towards the room."

"Yes mommy"! Isis yelled.

"I know you heard me calling you." Chante smiled and kissed me on the cheek.

"Get down from there and eat your breakfast."

I placed Isis on the ground and she headed to the kitchen. I wrapped my arms around my woman and whispered in her ear.

"Would you be my breakfast?"

"Oh my! You are so nasty." She giggled.

"But I'm serious Babe. I'm hungry." I said and kissed her on the neck.

"Not with Isis up and around."

"But she's in the kitchen." I nibbled on her ear.

"And what about when she is done eating?" she breathed. I knew her left ear was one of her spots.

"I can pop in one of her kid movies that ought to keep her occupied for a little while."

"But babe, we got to be at Ms. Cassie's at 10:30."

"Boo, it's not even 9:00 yet. So just be naked on that bed when I get back."

Chante did as she was told. I watched her remove her shirt and bra before I closed the bedroom door and headed to the living room.

"What are you doing, Yung?" Isis was still working on her toast and scrambled eggs.

"I'm looking for the Little Mermaid."

"Really? That's my favorite." Isis jumped up and down.

"I know princess. I thought you might want to watch this. So when you get finished eating, you can watch it."

"I'm ready now." Isis smiled. She drank the rest of her orange juice, grabbed her pink blanket and headed to the living room. I made my way back to the bedroom and locked the door. Chante was naked as I had requested.

"Daddy like." I licked my lips.

"You are so silly." she smiled.

"I love you." I made my way to the bed.

"I love you too."

"I wanna ask you something." I kissed her inner thighs.

"What babe?" Chante moaned from enjoyment.

"I want you to have my baby."

Before she could respond, I sucked on her clit and inserted my index finger in and out of her hot juicy pussy. The speedy vibrations of my tongue always made my baby squirt.

"Oh yes baby." She moaned.

"You gonna have my baby?"

"One day." She breathed.

I rubbed my rock hard, eight inch dick against Chante's pussy.

"Put a rubber on babe." She whined.

"Make love to me baby." She nibbled on my ear.

I put Chante's legs over my shoulders and stared into her honey brown eyes.

"I love you girl." I felt the sweat rolling off of my forehead.

"I love you too. I think I'm about to cum." She looked into my eyes.

"Oh baby. I'm cummin' too." I moaned.

I felt my body explode and I thought about some of my soldiers safely swimming into Chante's womb. I know it might take a couple times but I'm fully committed to this routine for the next two weeks.

"Oh my God." Chante whispered as I climbed off of her.

"It's 9:35." I said as I made my way into the master bathroom.

"Oh, let me freshen up and be on my way. I have to get started on this damn party."

"I'm sure it won't be that bad." I admired her naked body as she washed up and got dressed.

"Yung, stop looking at me like that." she blushed.

"I can't help that I love what I see." I wrapped my arm around my fully dressed baby. I rubbed my limp but easily aroused dick on her butt.

"Stop it now." Chante headed for the door.

"You know I have to go."

"I love you baby. I will see you later."

"I love you too. You are so mean."

"Uh huh." I winked.

Chante made her way to the living room. She had to convince Isis that she could watch her movie over her grandma's house. They left the house by 9:50. It generally took about twenty to twenty-five minutes to get to Ms. Cassie's house. Byron stayed on the next street over from his parents and I bet him and Marcie would be late getting to the party. I didn't want to deal with that drama. Chante said she was helping with the setup of the party and then she was

84

leaving. Isis is staying with her grandma for the night.

I heard the phone ring.

"Hello momma."

"Uh huh and where have you been lately?"

"There you go."

"Chante must be holding you hostage over there."

"Awe, is my number one girl getting jealous?"

"Boy don't play with me! When are you coming over here?" Momma yelled.

"I don't know Momma"

"Well, if I don't see you tomorrow, I'm coming over there."

***

I made love to Chante two more times when she made it back home. Chante leaned against the wall that I recently had her posted on. "Baby, what are you trying to do to me?"

"I just love you baby."

"I'm staying away from you for the rest of the day."

"Oh really?" I raised my eyebrow.

"You know I'm just playing." Chante stood in front of me with her hand on my dick.

"Alright now." I moaned.

"Alright what?" Chante sat on the toilet seat, never removing my dick from her hands. She molded it like a piece of clay as I moaned from enjoyment.

"Why are you teasing me boo?"

"Oh you like to tease people but they can't tease you?"

She continued to massage my dick and blow on the head of it.

"Girl, stop playing."

I picked her up and placed her on the bathroom sink. She didn't stop me or ask me about a condom this time. I banged her harder than I ever had before. We both screamed and shouted from pure ecstasy.

"This one is a baby maker." I sucked on the back of her neck.

"Boy stop playing."

"And what's so wrong with that?" I said feeling kind of hurt.

"I was just saying babe."

"Just saying what?" I crossed my arms.

"Nothing boo." she said and kissed my cheek.

I still felt a little hurt as we both washed up and put on our clothes.

"I think I am going to go holla at Mooch for a little while." I looked for my keys.

"Oh yeah." Chante handed me the keys that fell off of the dresser.

"I guess I will just take a nap or something." she said grabbing the remote and flicking through the TV channels.

"I won't be gone long." I kissed her on the forehead and left.

I thought about calling Mooch or Marco to see if they were home. I wanted to get out of the house. I didn't like to be around my boo when I was mad or upset. I guess that was just the man in me. I did my best to show my emotions when I'd first met Chante but now I found myself hiding how I really felt at times.

"Sup cuz?" Mooch had some rap music playing in his background.

"Are you at home?"

"Yeah man! We are having a little get together." He yelled

"So y'all got some hoes?"

"Basically." Mooch laughed.

"How many?"

"It's five over here."

"That's whassup. I'm outside right now." I said as I pulled up at his apartment.

"The door is unlocked."

Chapter Nine

The next couple of weeks were the same routine. Chante and I had sex three times a day and each time, I busted in her. Every day I kept wondering if today was the day that I got Chante pregnant. Why is that? It was because I wanted to make my mark in the world. I was twenty five years old. That was a good enough age to start a family. I was with the woman I love, so why not?

"Baby," Chante shouted.

"Sup babe?"

"You must've really been thinking over there." Chante held her stomach as she made her way to the bathroom.

"What's wrong babe?"

"I dunno. I guess I shouldn't have eaten all that spicy food last week."

I prayed she was pregnant. "Aw babe, do you want me to get you some Sprite from the fridge?"

"Would you babe?" She replied from the bathroom door.

"Has your period come on?" I asked. I knew she was usually due around this time. Having been with Chante for over a year; I was used to her cycle.

I could hear Chante throwing up.

"Not yet babe. If not today, maybe tomorrow."

"Yea, maybe tomorrow."

It had been four weeks straight of sexing her without real protection. Chante was always accurate when it came to her periods. I kept track of it in my mind. I made my way back to the bathroom with the Sprite. Chante was cradled by the toilet, hugging it.

"Is there anything I can do for you?"

"I dunno. I just don't feel well."

"Maybe it's because your period is almost here." I helped her to her feet and led her to the bed.

"I do sometimes feel a little queasy around this time but I've been feeling bad all week."

"Lay down babe. I will go fix you some soup and get you more Sprite. I will take care of you."

"Thanks boo. I don't know if I can keep it down."

I had convinced myself that Chante was pregnant. My plan was definitely in motion. I just wondered how long it would be before she decided to check things out. It didn't matter to me if I had a boy or a girl. I just wanted more than anything to have a baby by the love of my life.

Just then Marco called.

"What up Cuz?"

"You got it."

"What are you doing in a couple hours?"

I could tell Marco was in his car. I could hear the wind blowing and the music playing in his background.

"Probably nothing." I turned on the stove and put the Chicken noodle soup in a sauce pan.

"You need to come by the crib later."

"Why is that?" I asked.

"Aw man we are going to be doing it up over here later. You know?"

"Yeah. I might come by."

"I'm outside your crib right now. Let me holla at you for a second."

Marco knew I hated guys just showing up at my spot like that. So he better have a good reason for coming by. I put the soup on low and opened the front door. Marco was sitting inside his car; so I walked over to him.

"Dude, I thought I told you not to just run up at my crib like that. I got a lady and her daughter. You know I don't play that shit."

"I know that. I gotta make a run by the East Side Barbershop. You wanna ride?" Marco showed me the nicely rolled swisher behind his ear

This could finally be my chance to see whassup with Byron. I just wanna see where his mind was. Let's see if he's so quick to bring up my baby's name while I'm over there.

"Hold on a minute. I will be right back."

I had to take the soup to my sick baby. I wanted to check on her and see how she was doing. I put some saltine crackers on a plate with the soup. As I made my way into the bedroom, I noticed that Chante was asleep.

I kissed her on her forehead and she slowly opened her eyes.

"Baby, here's your food. I'm gonna ride out with Marco for a minute. But you call me if you need anything."

Chante shook her head and closed her eyes. I decided to call Shannon and tell her to stop by in an hour and check on her. Chante trusts my sister. If she thinks she might be pregnant; she'd tell my sister. And of course, my sister would tell me. I grabbed an ice cold beer out of the fridge and made my way to Marco's car.

"Bout time, cuz. I thought you weren't coming."

"I had to check on my girl."

"Is she ok?"

"She has been feeling kind of sick lately."

"Damn, I hope you didn't get her pregnant.. I stay strapped. I don't want any babies right now."

I didn't respond. I just nodded because I'm ready for a baby and I hoped Chante had my baby inside of her.

"So why are you headed to the east side?" I changed the subject.

"Oh, I just need some new movies and video games. You know they have great quality there."

"Yeah right and what else?" I knew there was more to it than that.

"There's this chick that works at the gas station next to the barbershop. I have been wanting to holla at her."

"I knew it," I laughed.

"You probably know her. You know fine ass Sherri from the PJs."

"Sherri?" I knew her mouth very well. "Yeah I know who she is but I never sexed her."

"That's whassup then." Marco smiled.

What he didn't know was that I was getting her to suck my dick every other week on her days off. Sherri is my pro. I first met her at one of the neighborhood gas stations. I got the number, talked to her, brought her to cuz's crib before Marco was in the picture, and got some great dome. Anytime I wanted it; I could get it. I couldn't wait to see the look on her face when we walk in the store. She knew the game. Act like we don't really know each other because I have a woman.

We pulled into the BP parking lot which was pretty empty at the time. When we made our way into the store, Sherri was at the register. I glanced at her and walked directly to the beer section. I could feel her eyes watching me.

"Whassup boo?" Marco approached Sherri's register.

"Nothing much." Sherri smiled. Her dimples showed as she ran her fingers through her micro braids.

"When are you gonna let me take you out on a real date?" Marco licked his lips.

"When you get serious and stop playing."

"I'm serious now. I wanna put twenty dollars on pump seven and you can keep the rest." Marco put a fifty dollar bill on the counter. "

"Oh I see big baller over here." Sherri put the thirty dollars in her shirt pocket. "

"I'm just letting you know that I will do you right." Marco ran his fingers down Sherri's honey brown neckline and lightly touched her breast.

"Yeah Sherri. Stop being so hard on the boy and let him take you out." I said as I made my way to the counter.

"You think I should?" Sherri raised her eyebrow.

"Yeah. He is a good dude and I will vouch for him."

"See there. My cousin vouches for me." Marco gave me a high five.

Sherri looked as if she had seen a ghost when he said the word "cousin"

"I see." she replied.

"I'm gonna call you in an hour and see whassup."

"Alright Marco." Sherri was eye balling me.

"That girl wants me." Marco said heading to the gas pump.

"Oh yeah" I saw I had a text message from Sherri.

It read 'Whassup?'

"This dick, when you goin' let me get some?" I responded.

"When is your next break?"

"In ten minutes."

"Meet me in the men's bathroom."

"Ok."

"Cuz, I'm heading to the barbershop. Damn, here comes the GM of this BP. Let's head to the shop, that bitch can't stand me."

"Why is that?" I asked.

"Because I banged her daughter at a party and she found out about it. She is trying to say that I turned her daughter out."

"Damn Cuz." I looked at my phone. Sherri said she had clocked out and was waiting for me in the bathroom.

"I'm gonna meet you over there. I gotta use the bathroom."

"You're not sick are you? Maybe you and Chante have a stomach virus." Marco laughed.

"Maybe so, but I will meet you over there."

"Alright."

Marco drove across the street as I entered the men's bathroom. Sherri had put paper towels on the toilet seat before sitting on it.

"Took you long enough? Why would you bring up the fact that you and Marco are cousins?" She pouted.

"Don't worry about that. You can worry about this." I pulled my dick out and rubbed it in her face.

Sherri deep throated me as I played with her D-cup breasts. I loved the way she played with my balls while I fucked her mouth. She spit me out, spit on the head and sucked the spit off.

"Can I feel that dick, boy? I got a dollar for one of those condoms on the bathroom wall."

"Girl, you know I can't fit that shit, but I got a Magnum in my pocket."

I did have a Magnum XL in my wallet. Not from the batch I use on Chante. I have a real batch for the hoes. I did wanna fuck Sherri just to see what that pussy was like. We had been dealing for about six months now. I bent her over the toilet pulling down her pants and sheer pink panties. I stuffed her panties in her mouth. I looked at her neatly shaved pussy. Those fat lips were hard to resist and I massaged her clit with my index finger. She was so wet. Smelling my fingers, I was happy she had no offensive odor. She grabbed the toilet bowl and spread her legs farther apart and I continued to play with her clit. Curiosity had the better of me and I wanted to taste her. I got down on my knees and sucked on her clit. I could hear her muffled moans. I put on the condom and eased my eight inches inside of her. Sherri felt good but I wanted her mouth on me.

"Let me cum in your mouth." I pulled the condom off. She spit out her panties and started sucking on me again. I rubbed on her breasts until I felt myself about to nut.

"Oh shit girl." I felt it squirt out and she caught it all.

My dick was still a little hard. I turned her back over and started pushing myself in her ass. She let me stick the head in, so I dug a little deeper. I put her panties back in her mouth and started humping like crazy. I put Sherri on the bathroom wall because the toilet was making too much noise.

Knock Knock

"Who is it?" I yelled out of panic, but maintained my stroke as I played in Sherri's pussy.

"It's me cuz. Are you ok?"

"Yeah. Be out in a minute. Go on with that shit." I continued stroking

"Ok. I was just checking on you."

"Man, I will be over there in a minute." I sped up my pace.

"Alright cuz."

I power drilled her juicy ass. I could hear her muffled cries even though her mouth was stuffed. That shit turned me on. I bit her on the back of her neck and just latched on to it, while I continued to finger fuck her pussy.

"Cum on my finger and cum on this dick," I whispered.

I could hear her muffled cries and I felt my fingers get soaking wet. I inserted another finger; penetrating all of her. I came so hard. I noticed she was still moaning, so I removed my dick from her ass and inserted my finger. I knelt back down and sucked on her pussy. Sherri did taste good.

"Cum girl," I whispered as I continued to eat her and play in her ass.

I suddenly felt her knees shake and I tasted her sweet nectar.

"Damn girl, you better not suck my cousin's dick like you do mine."

"You are trippin'," She laughed.

"I'm serious." I posted her back on the wall and fingered her pussy as she tried to pull up her pants. I stared deep into her eyes as she began to bite her bottom lip. I played with her clit until she came. I slowly removed my finger and placed it in her mouth. We tongue wrestled as she stroked my throbbing dick. I grabbed both her hands as I kissed her down below. It was odorless and sweet as I fucked her with my tongue. I picked her up and she wrapped her legs around my neck.

"I won't daddy. I promise I won't," She moaned.

I washed my face. I rinsed my mouth out in the sink and put two sticks of gum in my mouth.

"You better not. And don't let me find out that you did. Because if I find out I'm cutting you off. Let him do you, but you do me and only me."

"Ok daddy. Do you want it right now?"

"Don't you have to clock back it or something?"

"Naw I'm off work. I just told your cousin I had to work longer. Plus, he doesn't know where I parked my car. It's a block down the road, over my aunt's house." She pulled my limp dick out.

"Stop, I gotta go before my cuz comes back over here."

Sherri rose to her feet, washed her face and put her pants on.

"So when will you holla at me Yung?"

"I don't know. You know I got a woman." I shrugged my shoulders.

"Yeah I know." She straightened her hair.

"I will text you and let you know whassup. You know I will."

I decided to leave out of the bathroom first. I told her to count to sixty before walking out; just to make sure things didn't look obvious.

My cell started ringing. It was my sister, Shannon. Apparently I had a couple of missed calls.

"Sup sis?"

"Sup? Where have you been? I called you twice." Shannon was sounding panicky.

"Why and whassup?" I tried to remain calm.

"I just left Chante."

"And how is my baby doing?"

"Your baby." Shannon paused.

"Your baby is acting like she might be having a baby. She can't keep any food down. She said her period is a couple days late. I told her to buy a pregnancy test next week if her period isn't on by then."

"What did she say?" I smiled as I made my way to the barbershop.

"She said you wanted a baby right now and she wanted to wait. Is that true, bruh, You want a baby?"

"Yes sis, I really do want one."

Chapter Ten

Damn. I didn't know a pregnant woman went through so many emotions. We found out that Chante was having a baby girl. I was so excited, but I wish she would stop going being so emotional.

"Boo, are you almost ready?" I yelled from the living room.

Today I had a surprise for Chante. Since she did the honor of carrying my first born, I decided to get us a house. No child of mine was going to grow up in a place they will never own. I found a nice four bedroom, two and a half bath red brick house a few blocks down from our apartment. I didn't have a lot of credit; you can't put hustler down as a source of income, but my Momma agreed to sign for the house.

The former owners were members of my momma's church. They cut me a sweet deal and only wanted $90,000 for the house. I gave momma $45,000 upfront because I didn't want to be paying on a house forever. The neighborhood was quiet and there was plenty of yard space for a good barbecue grill and playground set for the girls. The home was in good condition and ready for us to move right in. I figured we could move next month when Chante's lease was up on the apartment.

Chante appeared in the doorway with her hands on her widened hips. Her face, along with everything else, had gotten plump in all the right places. She was sexier now that she was pregnant.

"Yeah Babe" she said looking miserable.

"Awe," "What's wrong with my girls?" I went over and rubbed her belly.

"This girl won't stay off of my bladder. I keep running to the bathroom."

"Alright Victoria. Let up on your Momma for a little while. I got something to show her."

"What are you talking about Babe?"

"Come on so I can show you." We headed to the car.

"While we are out, can we stop and get something to eat? I want some fried dill pickles with ranch dressing and a catfish sandwich with extra tomatoes and tartar sauce."

"You know my girls get whatever they want." I kissed Chante on her chubby left cheek and pulled off.

"Is that right?"

"You should know that by now. All of my girls, Isis included, can get whatever they want from me. I love you, Isis and Victoria with all of my heart. I would die for any one of you."

"Babe, now why do you want to make me cry? I just wanted to get something to eat. And a thick chocolate shake."

"I love you girl." I laughed and stopped in front of the house.

"Why did you come over here? Do you know someone that stays over here?" Chante looked up and down the street.

"I do now."

"What do you mean?" Chante looked puzzled.

"Well, next month, when your lease is up, we are moving into that house." I gently caressed her soft and silky face.

"What? Stop playing."

"I'm serious. I bought that house for our family. I want us to have a firm foundation. You know how much I love you and you know I'm going to marry you someday."

Chante leaned over and planted a juicy kiss on me.

"Oh my God. I love you so much. You make me so very happy." She cried.

"You've made me so very happy. And you will be daddy's little princess." I said leaning down to kiss her belly.

"I can't believe you actually bought a house baby. When do you get the keys? Can we take a look inside?"

I pulled the keys out of the glove compartment. "Yes baby. I got the keys. We can move in at any time. I just figured we should wait until the lease is upon your apartment."

"You really thought of everything." she said giving me a kiss.

"Yes Babe, I see the bigger picture. It has four bedrooms so Isis and Victoria can have their own rooms. I know my sisters liked their own space. Plus, we have an extra room."

"Uh huh. And what's that for?"

"What do you think baby? Another baby at some point in time."

"You are trippin' Victoria hasn't made it here yet and you are already talking about another baby?" She laughed.

"I'm just saying. Not right now but later on."

"Uh huh. Well we can look at this house a little later because I have to pee. I love our house though."

"Let me go and get my girls something to eat before I get cussed out again for no reason," I laughed and started the truck

***

My baby could put away some food. I loved to watch her eat. She made some of the same faces when we made love. My momma and sisters had been calling me. Everyone was so excited because I was having a baby. All of them wanted to babysit, even April. I had not really talked to my dad in a while. I was thinking about giving him a call.

"Baby, can I get a fish sandwich, fried dill pickles with ranch dressing and a chocolate shake to go? That was so good. I think I wanna eat that again later." Chante wiped her mouth with a napkin

"Whatever you want Babe."

"Thanks" Chante took another bite of her sandwich.

"Oh no. Now I have to go to the bathroom."

"It's to the right. Do you want me to go with you?"

"I got it." She made her way to the end of our row and I watched her enter the restroom before I sat back down.

I heard the familiar buzzing from my pocket. I'd had the phone on vibrate. I looked down at my phone; it was an out of area call.

"Hello."

"Whassup Yungsta?" It was Morgan.

Now remember I told y'all a while back that Big Earl, the dude I made runs for, had a daughter that I was banging? Well, that's Morgan. If I wasn't worried about being killed by her daddy, Morgan would have been my wifey. Twenty-two years old, caramel skin, hazel eyes, shoulder length sandy brown hair, five foot seven, and about 140 pounds. Did I mention booty like DAMN! I was getting hard just thinking about her sweet pussy.

"Sup Mo?" I tried to sound cool.

"Back in town for the summer, so you know whassup."

"You know I'm staying with a chick now. I can't just leave when I want to." I stood up from the table and walked outside of the restaurant.

"Yeah, I heard daddy saying something about you haveE a baby on the way, but I had to abort ours. Remember that?"

She always had to bring that shit up. Two years ago, we slipped up and she got pregnant. I was doing runs for her daddy and he would've killed me if he knew I had knocked her up. I had to do what was best and she knew that.

"I remember. How could I ever forget?"

"I'm just saying. You can find some time. She ought to be either eating or sleeping all the time by now."

"How would you know?"

"I got plenty of sisters. My daddy has like twelve kids. Only me and my three brothers are by my momma."

"Oh wow." I said shaking my head.

"Yeah, so I know you can find some time. My daddy was a woman pleaser too."

"I ain't got it like your daddy," I laughed.

"Well, I wanna see you. When can you make that happen?"

"Later on today. I'll call you."

"Ok, I can't wait to see you."

She hung up. I decided to finish the half of a cigarette I had from earlier.

"Babe." Chante made her way to the front door.

"Yes boo."

"I should have known you was out here smoking. I was sitting at the table waiting on you."

"Did you order the food that you wanted?" I asked as I put the cig back out

"Yes, I put the rest of your food in a to-go box and I'm waiting on the order."

"Are you ready to go?"

"Yeah, I'm ready to take a walk around the block, take a bath, talk to Isis and take a nap."

"It looks like you and Victoria have your afternoon and evening planned."

"That's what we are doing for the night."

"Are you hanging with the fellas later?" she asked.

"Probably so, but you know I won't be out late. And I will be calling to check on you like I always do." I said cool and relaxed

"I know babe. I just figured you might want to get out of the house for a little while. You always come back with some funny stories about your folks." She was so trusting.

I smiled and thought about seeing Morgan naked.

Chante headed for the truck with her doggy bag in hand.

"Well, come on so we can get home. I'm feeling kind of tired and I'm ready to lay down."

Chapter Eleven

Morgan, Morgan, Morgan.

That girl and me had some definite history and chemistry. I had really put her in the back of my mind after she left for college but I had to make sure things were okay at home before I decided to leave the house.

"Do you need anything else baby?" I pulled down the covers on our king sized bed and fluffed her pillows

"I'm good. I'm just going to wait on Isis to get off of the school bus."

"Alright, I'm going to take off for a minute but I will check on you later."

I headed to my truck. I called Mooch. I needed to see who was at his crib.

"Sup cuz?" Mooch said when he answered the phone.

"I'm headed to your spot. Who all is over there?"

"Just me. Marco rode with some homeboys to Florida for the week. He won't be back until next Sunday."

"I got someone I wanted to holla at."

"So I guess Morgan called you?"

"How did you know?"

"I ran into her this morning at the gas station. She was asking about you." "She called me while I was at a restaurant with Chante."

"So, what are you going to do since your former boo is in town?"

"She is probably just staying for a week or so, I'm gonna try to spend some time with her."

"I bet."

"I'm pulling up now." I said putting my truck in park.

"Ok, the door is unlocked."

I made my way into my old spot. Mooch was sitting in the living room drinking a beer.

"So, how are you feeling?" Mooch raised an eyebrow.

"What do you mean?" I knew what he was saying.

"I know you. I know all the shit that you have been through with Morgan. And now you got a baby on the way with Chante. I just hope you can handle all of this." Mooch handed me a beer

"I'm good Cuz."

Morgan was still in my heart and probably always will be. I decided to hit her up and she answered on the first ring.

"What's good Yungster?"

"You," I replied.

"No doubt, so where are you?"

"I'm at Mooch's crib."

"Oh ok. I see you managed to make it out of the house."

"Yeah." I hoped she wasn't going to stress the issue that I had a woman.

"I should be there in a few minutes."

"Aight,"

I hung up the phone. The look on my face must have upset my cousin a little bit.

"Everything ok?

"I guess," I said and patted my head.

"I see what you were saying. I just hope I'm doing the right thing by seeing Morgan. I don't want any drama right now. I will always have love for Morgan but I'm in love with Chante."

"I feel you, Yung. I think you should have parted ways with Morgan. Why re-open that can of worms. You feel me?"

In no time, we heard a knock on the door.

"I hear you, but it's a little too late for that. Morgan is at the door."

I felt my palms begin to sweat and my heart was racing as I opened the door.

"I thought you wasn't gonna let me in." Morgan stood there with her hands on her hips. Her hair was freshly curled. She was wearing a white wife-beater and some skinny blue jeans with all black pumps.

"How have you been?" I reached in and gave her a hug. She smelled like lavender and cotton candy.

"I'm doing ok. How have you been, Mooch?" Morgan said giving me a kiss on the cheek

"I'm doing well. Why didn't you bring a friend for me?"

"My bad, I got you next time."

"Is that right?" I raised an eyebrow.

"Yeah. Can I talk to you in the back for a minute?" She winked.

Morgan grabbed my hand and we made our way to my old bedroom. I still had the bed and dresser in there, you know, just in case I ever needed a place to crash.

"I would try to beat around the bush, but you know that's not my style. I've been dreaming about riding that dick since I made it to town."

"Girl, you know you are wild." I kissed her and began caressing her hard nipples.

"I missed you so much, Yung."

I didn't want to respond to that, so I continued kissing Morgan as she lay naked on the bed. She loved to be teased before sex.

"Why are you playing?" She moaned as I was kissing her inner thigh. I know what she wanted, this tongue. I massaged her clit with my index finger as I watched her sway her hips, she was so ready for me. I tasted her sweet nectar as I had done so many times, gently massaging her breasts as she moaned in ecstasy.

"You gonna cum for me, baby?" Morgan loved when I talked dirty to her. I did turn her out. She claimed I was the second dude she slept with. Seems like only yesterday she was seventeen and I was twenty one.

"Yes baby, oh here it comes."

I felt her body shake and I licked up all of her juices.

"Oh boy," She climbed on top of me and started massaging my dick.

"I'm ready for him now."

"Oh yea? Well, let me see if you still know how to handle him."

Morgan climbed her sexy caramel body on top of mine and sat on my pipe. That pussy still gripped my dick and it was soaking wet.

"You know I can ride this thing." Morgan smiled and licked her own breast. She knew that shit turned me on. She rode it slow at first before picking up some speed. Morgan leaned down on my chest and began nibbling on my ear. I grabbed both of her butt cheeks and jiggled them. Morgan continued to grind on my dick like a pro.

"How does that feel baby?" She moaned.

"You know it feels good," I closed my eyes as she sucked on my neck.

"You goin' nut for me, boo?"

"Not yet, you know I got to hit that from the back." I said flipping her over.

I fingered her ass as she continued to moan. I parted both of her cheeks and licked on her pussy. She let out a loud whimper.

"Give it to me, boo. I wanna feel you inside of me."

Without her paying attention, I slipped on a good Magnum XL and power drove that pussy. I love the way Morgan brought her ass back on my dick...so I don't have to do all the work. I taught her well.

"Here I come baby. Oh shit."

I gently kissed Morgan on her soft and tender back.

"Yung, why you tryna start me back up?"

"I wasn't boo." I wiped the sweat from my eye.

Morgan looked for her shirt and bra on the bedroom floor. "I really missed you." Morgan said as she looked for her shirt and bra on the bedroom floor

"So that's it. You just been missing this pipe?" I handed her a bright blue pair of panties

"Yes, but that's not all and you know that."

"Uh huh." I looked for my boxers and shorts.

"So, are we gonna chill for a minute or do you have to go?" Morgan stopped at the doorway before heading to the bathroom.

I looked at my phone, no missed calls and it was only 4 p.m.

"I'm good. I'm gonna be over here for a minute. Whassup?"

"I was just asking."

I followed Morgan into the bathroom and turned on the shower; she washed up in the sink.

"Oh, it's like that?" She smiled as she watched me get naked.

"You are silly. That was a workout. I just figured I would take a shower."

108

"Can I join you?"

"I guess so." I said feeling a little unsure. I had to make sure that when we had sex, I pulled out in time. I couldn't afford to get her knocked up again. This time I had to be smart.

"You goin' let me hit you in your butt this time?"

"Yung," she whined.

"Come on Morg. We are in the shower so let's get freaky."

"It just hurts so badly. You be forgetting how big you are."

"I promise I will be gentle." I made my way in the shower and waited on Morgan to join me. She covered her head with a plastic bag.

"Don't be looking at me crazy. You know I don't play about my hair."

"I know boo. I know, but bend that juicy booty over here so I can blow your back out."

"Very funny." She spread her legs, put her hands on the shower wall and jiggled that juicy booty. The combination of hot water and juicy booty made for a twenty minute round two in the shower.

Just as we finished and were catching our breath, there was a knock on the bathroom door.

"Quit playing Mooch." I knew it was his hatin' ass.

"Nigga, don't be running up my water bill. You had a phone call."

I dried off, put my clothes back on and headed in the bedroom to find my phone. Chante had called.

"Hello." I replied as I was looking for my socks.

"Hey babe, what are you doing?"

"Nothing much. What are my girls doing?"

"Nothing, we're all piled up in the bed watching some movie."

"Sounds exciting."

109

Morgan entered the room. I could tell she was a little annoyed by the fact that I was on the phone. I walked past her and made my way to the living room and sat next to Mooch on the couch.

"I guess so. Oh, excuse me." She burped.

"It's cool babe." I laughed and shook my head

"Well, I didn't want anything. Tell Mooch that I said hello."

"Ok babe." I was happy to be ending the conversation because I figured Morgan would be coming in here very soon.

"Mooch, Chante says hello."

"Tell her I said whassup."

"I heard him, talk to you later."

"Later; I love you."

"I love you."

I was able to end the call before there was any drama.

"Man, you are playin' with fire. You might get burned. Be careful," Mooch whispered.

"Stop tryin to jinx me. I'm handling mine." I was pissed.

At that moment, Morgan walked into the living room. She was fully dressed and on her phone.

"Well what time was you gonna be ready?" Morgan sat down beside me on the love seat and propped her legs on my lap.

"Uh huh...around 8 p.m? Oh...yeah...sounds good. I will see you then."

"You goin' let me meet some of your friends?" Mooch gave Morgan a wink.

"Yeah. When I talk to one of them. That was a guy I met at a barbecue of my dad's. It was a couple weeks ago and I had forgotten about him." Morgan laughed.

"Oh yeah," I said trying not to look jealous. Still, I think my true colors were showing.

"What's wrong, Yung? I can't go out on a date but you can talk all lovey dovey with your bitch?" Morgan replied sarcastically.

"Whoa, first off, Chante ain't no bitch. Ok? You don't have to call her out of her name. Second, you can go out with whoever you want. Well, as long as I don't know them." ," I stood to my feet, I felt my blood boiling.

"What? So, if I said I knew Chante; then what?" She rolled her eyes.

"Do you?" I already knew the answer to that question.

"I'm just saying."

"But you don't. But if you did, no, I wouldn't be with her. I have never been with any of your friends and you know that."

"Yeah, it better stay that way because I don't play that."

"Girl stop." I gave her a kiss.

***

Morgan left Mooch's crib so she could get ready for her date. I tried not to be mad but I really was. I know I didn't have the right to be mad, but I do have feelings for Morgan and that wasn't going to end just because of Chante.

"You aiight?" Mooch must've noticed the confused look on my face.

"I don't know, I didn't realize that I still had all these feelings for Morgan. I just been so focused on Chante and the baby. But when I chilled with Morgan today, shit just came up." I said honestly.

Mooch lit a cigarette. "See man, I told you that you are playing with fire. I don't think you need to go there with Morgan anymore."

"You know that's gonna be hard. You know how Morgan is. She likes to get her way. Up until now, she has always gotten her way with me. I just don't know what I'm gonna do."

Mooch went in the kitchen and brought back two beers.

"I told you fam. Talk to her if you want, but you have to draw the line somewhere. What would happen if Chante found out about all of this?"

"What do you mean?"

"I mean, mistakes happen. Y'all could be somewhere and possibly run into Morgan. You don't know how Morgan is going to deal with seeing you with your pregnant chick."

I calmed down as I popped open a can of beer.

"True, I'm just gonna try to make it through this week."

I felt my phone vibrating from a text message, it was from Morgan.

'No matter who I'm with...I will always want you more'

I just ducked my head because Mooch might be right about Morgan.

Chapter Twelve

After our reunion, Morgan had been texting me. I met up with her again at Mooch's crib again but couldn't stay long because Chante had been having a lot of contractions. We had been to the hospital, but her doctor wouldn't keep her because she wasn't dilated enough. The next week would really be touch and go.

I received another text from Morgan. She was telling me that she really wanted to see me. I waited until Chante and Isis was taking a nap before calling her back.

"Hello," I whispered.

"What's up?" Morgan replied.

"Chillin' at the house, I thought I told you I was gonna give you a call later." I said a little annoyed. "

"I know boo, but I was getting restless. I want to see you." She whined.

"I know that," I looked around to make sure no one was coming down the hall. I checked the bedroom and the girls were still sleeping.

"I been staying at the house to be with Chante and the baby."

"Has she been having problems?"

"She dilated a little bit. The doctor said the baby would be here in the next week or two." I couldn't believe I was having this conversation with Morgan. I could only imagine how this made her feel

"Well, I'm glad you are trying to do the right thing. I'm proud of you. Maybe if situations were different we could have..." she said, her voice trailing off.

"I know," I interjected. I just didn't want to make Morgan upset by my newfound happiness. "When are you going back to school?"

"I'm going back up there Sunday morning."

"Ok, it's only Thursday. We have time. Let me call my sister and then I will call you back."

"Alright."

She hung up. While I did want to spend some time with Morgan, I didn't want to leave Chante home alone. I decided to see what Shannon was doing. I knew she was on break from college.

I dialed Shannon's number.

"What up bruh?"

"What up sis? What are you doing right now?"

"Nothing much, just watching a movie with April and Lil' Ricardo."

"Oh, can you come over here for a little while?"

"Why and what's up?" She sounded concerned.

"I wanted to leave for a minute but I don't want to leave Chante by herself."

"What's wrong?"

"Nothing like that, the doctor just said that the next week is touch or go. I wanted to leave but I would rather someone be here."

"Oh ok, are you going to meet with someone?"

"Sis, can you just come over here right now? Yes or no?"

"I guess so, but I want details."

"Yeah, yeah, and don't say anything to April because she will just say something to momma."

"I got you bruh. I'm headed to my car right now,"

"Ok, thanks."

I decided to call Morgan since the girls were still asleep. I told her to meet me at Mooch's in about thirty minutes. I knew Mooch was at home so I sent him a text. He decided to call.

"Cuz, what's going on?"

"What are you talking about?"

114

"I thought I told you to chill out with this Morgan bullshit. You are going to have a baby very soon. What's the point? You know, usually I wouldn't comment on how you handle your business, but you're playing with fire."

"Man, the girl will be gone on Sunday. I'm not leaving Chante by herself; Shannon is coming over here. I'm not leaving until Shannon gets here and if anything goes on, I'm right down the road. You feel me?"

"Alright cuz. Do what you do. You're my family and I got your back. The door will be unlocked."

He hung up the phone. I knew he was right but I just couldn't say no to Morgan right now. A part of me wanted to see her; another part knew I had a responsibility to Chante. I'd made sure someone was there with Chante.

A short time later, Shannon arrived. I opened the front door to let her in.

"So what's up?" Shannon made her way to the couch.

"Damn, no hello or anything?"

"Stop playing! Who are you trying to meet? This better be good because normally you won't leave Chante." Shannon said with a straight face.

"It's Morgan."

"What? You mean to tell me that you are still dealing with her? That bitch could have got you killed. I'm not staying over here for her."

"Come on Sis," I knew she would react like this. Shannon saw the big picture. Morgan's father is a powerful man and could easily have me erased.

"The girl is leaving on Sunday. I'm not gonna be gone that long. Just do it for me, please."

115

"Why? You got all you need in that bedroom back there. What if Morgan is plotting against you? You know she had never gotten over that abortion. Think bruh."

"It's not like that," I refused to believe Morgan would do anything to hurt me.

"Just hurry up. Well, at least I can get a good meal. I know pregnant women keep the fridge filled." She headed to the kitchen.

"Thanks Sis."

I headed to my ride. I had two text messages from Morgan. She was at Mooch's crib; sitting in the living room and waiting on me. I knew I was wrong for sneaking off from my pregnant woman; but I wasn't ready to put Morgan all the way out of my life. I don't know why but that was the truth. I could only imagine what her and Mooch were talking about. I hope they weren't discussing me but I'm sure they were. I parked my truck and opened Mooch's front door.

"Hey, what's up?" Morgan grinned.

"What's so funny?" I gave them both an awkward glance.

"We are watching this comedy show on HBO. These niggas are funny."

"Oh ok." I relaxed a little bit. I was glad that my relationship was not the topic of their discussion.

Morgan stood to her feet and held out her hand. We made our way down the hall holding hands. I looked back in Mooch's direction, but he was giving all his attention to the TV.

"What's wrong?" Morgan pouted her lips. I hated it when she did that.

"Stop making that ridiculous face."

116

"You looked like something was wrong when you opened the door." Morgan sat on the edge of the bed.

"Everything is ok."

"If you say so."

We sat in silence as Morgan pulled out a bag of Kush and rolled a blunt. She passed it to me and I took a hit.

"Damn, where did you get that?" I coughed and gagged.

"From my Pops, you know he only has that strong shit."

I took a swig of some water she had in a cup.

"Yeah, I thought it might be relaxing and allow you to be at your freakiest."

"You're silly."

She was right. By the time we finished smoking, I felt like a million bucks. No worries and no problems. I remembered to turn my phone ringer on. No matter what, I had my daughter's birth on my mind.

Morgan lay back on the bed and started massaging her titties and rocking her hips. She removed her clothes slowly and looked at me seductively. She always knew the things that turned me on. Chante always seemed so timid with these things and Morgan was more outgoing. Morgan brought her index finger to her mouth and sucked on it while she rocked her hips. My dick was already hard. Eventually my hands started feeling parts of her body. I rubbed my middle and index fingers over her throbbing pussy lips. Morgan freely spread her legs apart. I vibrated those fingers over her clit and watched as her juices began to flow. I started to finger her pussy. She moaned, urging me to stroke her harder and faster. I did. Morgan rocked her hips back and forth while I fingered her. I was so turned on that I stopped and licked her juices from my fingers.

The taste of her sweet nectar was calling my tongue to her pot of honey. I devoured her pussy. I stuck my tongue in and out of her, wiggling my tongue on and around her walls as she screamed for more and more.

"Oh baby, I'm about to cum," she hollered

I wiggled faster and I licked up all her juices. I continued to suck on her clit until she came again. I put my index finger in her ass to widen it. I softly kissed her butt cheeks to relax her. Eventually, I managed to stick another finger in there without her usual complaints. Morgan loved every second of pleasure. I flipped her on her stomach and continued to play with her but my dick was throbbing. I couldn't take it anymore. I put my dick head in her ass and teased it. Morgan started rocking back and forth, forcing more of me inside her.

"I see you think you can handle me." I breathed.

"I can," She moaned.

"You think so, I don't want the neighbors to hear you. Let's go." I smiled as I slowly stroked her. I found her panties and placed them in her mouth.

I picked up the pace and really started stroking that ass. Morgan's moans turned to screams as she began to cum. I put a finger in her pussy. I felt her body shiver from delight and soon my hand was soaking wet.

"No one will ever give it to you the way I do. No one. This will always be mine. Oh shit babe, here I come."

We lay in the bed, covered in our own juices and overcome by the explosion that had occurred.

Morgan laid on my sweaty chest. I could feel my heart almost beating out of my chest. She began to run her fingers up and down my stomach. I reached on the table by the bed for my cigarettes and lighter. The first puff of the cigarette boosted my natural high. I could feel my dick beginning to harden. I looked at my phone; it was only 6:00. No one had called me yet. I assumed everything was ok.

"I really missed you, Victor. Things are so different now. Sometimes I think it's just over between us."

"Morgan, you'll always be special to me. I know things are different now, but I still made time for you. I wanted to see you."

"Will we be able to see each other again before I go?" She looked into my eyes.

"I don't know. I got a lot going on right now. It was hard for me to get away today."

Morgan sat up in the bed. "Oh, I guess you don't love me anymore. Now you just get at me whenever."

"Come on Morg." I continued lying back on the bed because I was still feeling a little weak. "You know what time it is. I'm doing the best that I can. I'm here right now, doesn't that mean anything?"

"I guess it should, but it's just not the same."

I sat up on the side of the bed. "I'm sorry, but this is my life right now. I still want us to be cool and chill when we can."

"But what if I wanted more?" Morgan stood at the door with her clothes in her hands.

"I can't get into that right now, but I'm telling you that I still want you in my life."

"I see, so, I guess I just have to settle for what I can get now."

She headed into the bathroom. I heard her lock the door and turn on the shower. I hated to hurt

Morgan, but what did she expect me to do? Turn my back on my child. I can't change what happened in the past and I'm not gonna act like I can do anything about it. I decided to call my sister and see what was up at home.

"What's up Sis?"

"It's about time. Is that tramp gone?"

"Don't start Shannon. What's going on over there?"

"Nothing much. Isis is up watching TV. I fixed her something to eat and Chante is still sleeping. When are you coming back over here?"

"I will be there in a minute."

"So, did you get to say goodbye to your friend?"

"Come on now, I don't say goodbye to friends. I only say 'see you later' and why are you sweatin' me? I got everything under control. Morgan knows what's up."

"Yeah, I just don't want anything to happen to you. You have a good thing at home."

"I know Sis. Believe me, I know." I smiled as I thought about Chante and the baby.

"Well, hurry up and get here. I got a life too, don't you know. I want to go see my boo."

"Girl stop," I laughed as I hung up the phone.

I didn't think I had been on the phone that long, but I no longer heard the shower running. I really needed to get in there before I made it home. I headed down the hall and was shocked to see the bathroom door open. Maybe Morgan went into the living room with Mooch but I didn't hear anyone talking. I walked in living room, but all I saw was Mooch.

"Where did Morgan go?" I asked.

"She left cuz. She's gone."

Chapter Thirteen

Damn! I felt bad about the way things ended with Morgan. The last thing I ever wanted to do was break her heart again. But I had to be real with her. I turned on the radio and 'Thin Line between Love and Hate' was blasting on the station. Honestly, hearing that song at that moment scared the shit out of me. Was that supposed to be a sign? Was God trying to tell me something?

I pulled up to my carport. Shannon and Chante's cars were parked side by side. I took a couple deep breathes and lit a cigarette as I walked in the front door. I smelled fried chicken and biscuits in the air and immediately felt more at ease. My home was my castle and I wasn't about to feel threatened here.

"Hey Yung, where have you been?" Isis ran into my arms and I picked her up for a hug. She kissed me on the cheek and I put her down.

"Just at my cousin's house, little lady." I smiled at how much that little girl loved me. I loved her just like a daughter.

"Ok, talk to you later."

She ran to her room to watch Snow White and the Seven Dwarfs. I could hear the dwarfs singing from her bedroom door. I went across the hall to the master bedroom. I opened the door and realized Chante must be awake. The bathroom light was on and the bed was a mess on one side.

"Are you ok in there, baby?" I headed toward the door.

"No, your daughter is laying on my bladder. I will be happy when she comes out." Chante whimpered.

I heard the toilet flush and the faucet running.

"Hopefully it won't be much longer. I can't wait to welcome Victoria Imani DaMone into this world."

I gently rubbed on Chante's swollen belly. I could feel our daughter moving around in there. I just couldn't imagine how that felt on Chante's end. She had a human being growing inside of her. I was thinking how amazing women were.

"Try not to talk so much," Chante moaned.

"Why is that Babe?" I looked puzzled.

"Because, Victoria kicks the most when she hears your voice."

"Daddy's little girl," I kissed Chante's stomach and I felt our baby kick.

"You see what I mean?"

I nodded but was amazed at the same time. My daughter was already familiar with my voice. It made me want to cry. My daughter, my seed. I would die for her and I had never even met her.

***

Two weeks later my beautiful princess made her way into this world. Three and a half of pushing but Chante made it through. I had never heard so many curse words flow from my woman's mouth. Chante had Victoria around that morning and the feeling didn't return to my hand until after noon. I had been holding her hand for support during labor. I couldn't believe the pussy could stretch that far. Damn. I have a new respect for women.

When the family arrived, I met them in the nursery and held up the baby for them to see. Momma looked at the card that read, 'Damone female child'. I gently kissed my daughter on her forehead, told her I loved her and placed her back in the hospital crib. I went out to see the family.

"Congratulations brother. This is a big day for you." April was all smiles

123

"Thanks sis," I grinned happy that April had something positive to say.

"Now you have a daughter, a future young woman. I just hope you teach her how to avoid men like yourself."

"Damn it April. We are not going to do this here." Momma snapped.

I yanked my hand from her grasp. A part of me wanted to slap her but she was right.

"It's cool Momma. April has a point for once. I'll make sure my daughter knows the difference between a good and a bad man."

"Anyways I just called Amari and she said she would be here this weekend." Shannon made her way in between Momma and April.

"Ok, it's been a while since I have seen my big sis. I don't know why she had to move five or six hours away from us."

"Momma, you know why."

"You know how momma is," April giggled.

"Well, momma doesn't have to worry about you going anywhere." I teased April.

"Shut up, Yung." April pouted.

"Stop it, Yung. April and any of you are welcome to stay with me as long as you want. I love all of my babies and my grandbabies too."

"We know Momma; y'all want to go see Chante?"

"Sure, if she's not sleeping. Maybe you should check on her first."

"Ok," I headed to Chante's hospital room. I heard her talking to someone.

"Hey Babe." I was shocked to see her ex, Byron, and little Isis.

"Hey Yung," Isis smiled and ran over to give me a hug.

"Hey sweetie," I said putting on a fake smile.

"Me and daddy came to check on mommy and I want to see my new sister. I'm so excited. First I had a baby brother and now I have a baby sister." Isis jumped up and down.

"Yung, can you take me to go see my baby sister?"

"Actually, I will take you, sweet pea. Congratulations, Yung." Byron rose to his feet and

Byron shook my hand. I know he really wasn't happy because I now had a baby with his ex. I was sure he wanted to sound pleasant because his little girl was in the room.

"Thanks man," I looked directly in his eyes. Our conversation was a long way from being over.

"See you later, Yung." Isis waved as she exited the room.

"Ok sweetheart," I waved as I made my way to Chante's bedside.

"Before you go off," Chante repositioned herself in her bed.

"Byron just brought Isis up here to see the baby. They hadn't been in here long before you came."

"I wasn't going to say anything, babe." I lied.

I would handle my beef with Byron. Chante just gave birth. I knew in my mind that she had to maintain a co-parent relationship with Byron because of their child.

"Really? I thought you would snap."

"I'm good." I gently kissed my woman on her cheek.

"My momma and sisters are in the nursery. They wanted to come see you if you are up to it."

"Of course. They should be bringing our baby in a few minutes."

"Ok baby, I'll go get them."

I saw Byron and Isis casually talking to my folks. I saw April rolling her eyes. No telling what the conversation was about; everyone knew Byron had a son by crazy ass Marcie.

"My sister is so little, daddy." Byron was holding Isis up to the glass.

"Was I that small?"

"Yes you were, princess," Byron laughed.

"Well, I got a lot of work to do."

"What do you mean, sweetie?" Shannon giggled.

"I have a brother and now I have a sister. That's a lot for a five year old. It's gonna be hard taking care of them both but I guess that's what big sisters do."

We all laughed at her excitement.

"Is Chante still up?" Momma smiled.

"Yes, she said she wanted you all to come see her."

"Ok," April and Shannon said in unison.

"Daddy can I go see mommy one more time before we go to McDonald's?" Isis hopped around on one leg.

"Yes sweetie," Byron nodded.

"Come on, Isis,. You can walk with me." Momma said taking her hand

I waited until all the women were out of sight before I spoke to Byron.

"Man to man, you are really starting to over step your boundaries, partner."

"What tha hell are you talkin' about? You're not the only man that has a baby by Chante. I got a five year old by her, remember? My daughter wanted to see her momma and her sister. Do you have a problem with that?"

"Don't try to play me, nigga. You know what I mean. Stay in your lane." I wanted to put his face through the glass but I was trying to keep my cool.

126

"I'm good, Yung. Marcie keeps me pretty busy. That crazy girl wants to try for another baby. You know she's pissed you and Chante have a daughter." Byron smiled.

"You can keep her crazy ass, and tell her to stop calling me."

"Man, I could care less. I gotta deal with her because of my son. I'm not trying to piss her off because she might try to get my child support raised. If she calls you, she calls you. I know you don't want her, so it doesn't matter to me."

"You're right. I don't want her but, you make sure you know that Chante is mine. I know y'all have a child together but make sure that's all you got. You feel me?"

Chapter Fourteen

I was enjoying being a daddy. I never knew I could love another person as much as I loved my 'Mani bug'. I found myself waking up when she cried for a bottle. I hadn't quite mastered changing her diapers but I was definitely trying my best. Victoria was almost 5 months old. Where did the time go? She looked just like me. We had the same brown complexion and big brown eyes. I loved her curly black hair and the way she smiled at me.

"Yung, can you fix me some cereal, please?" Isis asked. She was enjoying being a big sister. She loved to hold her and sing to her.

"Sure thing baby girl."

"Was my sister crying again?" Isis sat at the kitchen table making silly faces to Victoria. They both laughed.

"Yes, she had a stinky diaper." I smiled.

"Yuck, I will be glad when she can use the bathroom."

"Me too," We both laughed.

"I love the 1st grade. My teacher lets me go to the chalkboard and everything."

I sat Isis' cereal in front of her.

"That's great sweetie. You are such a big girl."

"Yes, I'm going to teach my brother and sister what I learned at school. They will be smart like me."

"You are such a good big sister."

"I know," She wiggled around in her seat as she ate her cereal.

"Is your mommy still asleep?"

"I think so." Isis wiped her mouth and headed to her room.

Chante was usually up by now. It's already 6:30 a.m., and Isis needs to wash up and get ready for the bus at 7:40 a.m. I made my way into the master bedroom with Victoria in my hand. The bed was a mess and I noticed the bathroom light was on.

"Are you ok baby?"

"Yes and no," I heard Chante flushed the toilet.

"What's wrong?" I saw the look on her face. She appeared to have been crying.

"I just can't believe this happened again." She was holding a pregnancy test in her hand.

"Are you serious?" I shook my head and looked at our daughter.

"Well, don't look at me. You played a part in this too."

"Well, I'm here baby. I guess we will have to be more careful the next time."

"Next time? How many times do you think I want to be pregnant? Victoria is five months old and I am probably a month pregnant right now. So when this baby is born, she'll be fourteen months old."

"Well, I know it was unexpected but the more the merrier. I will love this next baby just as much as I love Victoria and Isis."

"I love you so much baby, but I don't want any more after this. Carrying a baby takes a lot out of a woman. I just got back into my clothes and now I will be fat again." Chante kissed me gently as the baby made her way back into my arms.

"But you are always beautiful to me, baby." I kissed her.

"Thanks boo, but what about our finances? Do you think we'll be ok?"

"Of course," I said with confidence. We definitely had the room in our home. I'd paid for the house, so our only concern would be the utilities.

"We can afford another baby. I wonder if it will be another girl."

"I don't know, we might have Victor Isaiah DaMone."

***

Chante got Isis ready for school. I heard her talking to Isis about another baby. Isis seemed excited and she asked if it would be a boy or a girl. I decided to tell my folks in person because I would never get them off of the phone.

"I thought you was gonna be the baby a little bit longer. But daddy loves his little princess." I played with Victoria as she smiled.

Moments later, Chante entered the house.

"Do you feel ok baby?" I was concerned because Chante had so much morning sickness during the last pregnancy.

"Yea, I feel better because I know I'm pregnant. That explains why my period didn't come this month."

"Did you want to take the day off?"

"No, I might as well work as much as I can because I will be on maternity leave again in about seven or eight months."

"Ok. You could take off if you wanted to. You're working full-time and that might be too much."

"I can handle it; I have a nice desk job. So I won't be spending a lot of time on my feet."

"Well, I just thought I would ask. Me and the baby are going to Mommas a little later. I guess I will break the news to her."

"Yea ok, I know she will love that. Someone else for her to spoil."

"Yup, I'm surprised she hasn't called me yet."

"I'm sure she will." Chante kissed me.

"You better quit before you wake up your friend." I started to feel my nature rising

She put her hand in my boxers. "Oh yeah, I think it's too late. The damage has already been done."

"So it's my fault?" I pulled up Chante's shirt and began massaging her breasts. She removed her pants and panties.

"Yes, this is definitely your fault." She motioned me to the bed.

***

Chante made it out the door around 8:20 a.m. She wanted to make love, but I didn't want her to be late for work. I let my tongue do all the work. I figured I could get myself off after she left..

After reaching my climax and flushing it down the toilet; I noticed I had several missed calls. My mom called twice and Mooch called. I dialed Mooch's number because I knew what my mom wanted; the baby.

"What's up fam?" Mooch answered

"Nothing yet, I'm taking Victoria over my mom's in a few."

"You coming by after that?"

"What's up?"

"Boss man has to discuss another job with us. What time will you be available?"

"Can we meet around 1p.m?"

"I will hit him up and let him know, why so late?"

"Nigga, my daughter is taking a nap. She won't be up until around ten. Plus, you know my momma is gonna want to talk when I get over there. I have to tell her the news."

"Yea, auntie be trippin'. What news?" Mooch laughed.

"Chante is pregnant again. She took a pregnancy test this morning."

"Damn, you're not giving the coochie time to heal."

"Shut up It's mine." I hated when niggas said shit like that.

"Well, if you're happy, I'm happy. You got two kids like me now. So you know we got to get this paper."

"Right on," I agreed.

"Alright then,

After about forty-five minutes of slumber, daddy's little princess began to cry. I'd fixed two bottles, packed a half a can of formula, an extra outfit and some diapers in the diaper bag.

"Daddy's coming sweet baby," She wiggled around on her back, her face lighting up as I picked her up.

"Someone made a stink," I frowned. Victoria drooled and laughed.

I heard my phone ringing in my pocket.

I put my daughter in her crib, grabbed the diaper and wipes and looked at my phone. No surprise; it was my momma calling.

"Good morning Ma." I held the phone with my chin while I changed Victoria's diaper.

"Where are you at with granny's little angel?" she demanded.

I giggled as I threw the soiled diaper in the trash can.

"Your little angel took a shit. Daddy was cleaning it up."

"Oh well, I know you better get granny's baby over here before I send April over there to get her."

"We are on the way momma." I straightened up Victoria's clothes, picked her up and looked for my keys.

"I'm looking for my keys. I got something to tell you,"

"Something like what?"

"I will tell you when I get there with your little angel."

"Well hurry up, I will see y'all in a few."

The way my mother had taken to Victoria, I was sure she would welcome another baby and give him or her the same attention. I'm glad I have a Suburban, I thought to myself as I strapped her in the car seat. I have plenty of room for another car seat. I thought about getting Chante a four-runner or some type of SUV. That Camry wouldn't have enough room for two car seats and a six-year old. A friend of mine had a few SUVs for sale; I planned to go see him.

I pulled into my mother's car port and I saw the side door open. Momma came out the door with one hand on her hip. I barely cut off the engine when my she opened the back door.

"It's about time that you got here with my angel."

"Granny was coming over there to get her angel."

"Hello momma."

"Hello son," She smiled as she entered the door.

"I'm glad you noticed I was here." I frowned playfully.

Momma put the diaper bag in the kitchen and then she and Victoria sat in the living room. "Anyway, what did you have to tell me?"

Momma put her granddaughter in her bouncy bed; that would entertain her for a while.

"You are just straight to the point aren't you?"

"Boy, just say what you was going to say."

"Well, Chante found out that she is pregnant again."

"Are you serious? That girl is just beginning to heal from this baby.

"You need to slow it down, son."

"Really? That's not the reaction that I thought you would have."

"What?" Momma walked in the kitchen. She grabbed one of her cigarettes and lit it.

"You know I'm happy. I love Victoria and I will love the next one, but that's a lot on Chante's body. She is working and she just had a baby five months ago."

"I understand that momma. We were surprised too. But like I told Chante, the more the merrier. I'm not going anywhere." I gave her a hug.

"You really love her, don't you?" She looked deep into my eyes.

"Yes Momma, I really do. I love my daughter too and I would never harm them or leave them."

"My son, you've made me remember what true love is really about. Thank you for that."

"Anytime."

She walked back in the living room and picked up Victoria "You make sure you keep your promises to your family."

"I will."

"Ok, I guess you can go now. I want to spend some time with my angel. I might get April to take us grocery shopping in a little while. You make sure you leave the car seat in the garage."

"I could take you shopping. I didn't have anything planned until 1:00 p.m." I put the baby's bottles in the refrigerator

"That's ok baby, you tell Mooch I said hello because I'm sure that's where you are going."

"Ok, I will be back before 5:00 p.m."

134

I kissed my daughter and headed for the door. I looked down at my phone and noticed it was 11:00 a.m. I decided I would go over to Mooch's because I didn't have any other plans. I dialed his number

"Sup cuz?" Mooch answered

"I'm headed your way. Mom didn't need me. What are you up to?"

"You know me," Mooch laughed. I could hear female's voice in the background.

"Yeah, I know you."

Chapter Fifteen

I pulled up in the driveway of Mooch's crib, I noticed a familiar black Volvo. Mooch probably had some of our old college chicks at his spot. I pulled two condoms from my glove compartment just in case; and then headed to the front door and walked in.

"Whassup cuz?" I shouted toward the sound of music playing down the hall.

"We back here," Marco yelled back.

Marco was in my old room getting head from some redbone chick.

"My bad cuz."

"Oh you're good. Mooch is in his room with two broads." Marco slapped the chick on her ass.

"I'm gonna knock on his door before I enter," I laughed.

"Aiight." Marco lay back on the bed and I watched the girl's ass and neck move up and down. As I closed his door, I thought of Marco as a younger version of myself.

I knocked on Mooch's door.

"You decent in there?"

"No, but I'm sending one your way."

A white chick named Rachel opened the bedroom door. She was one of the usual freaks that came by and serviced us.

"What's up Yung?" She smiled as she led me into the living room and made herself comfortable on the couch.

"Why don't you come over here and join me."

"Ok," I said making sure the front door was locked and dimmed the lights. I was glad I grabbed my rubbers at the last minute.

"So what's up?"

"Whatever you like," Rachel took off her t-shirt and began massaging her large melon sized breasts.

"You gonna let me titty fuck?"

"Is that what you want?" She licked her lips seductively

"What did you have in mind?" I pulled out my eight inches and she started stroking it. Rachel teased the head of my dick with her tongue.

"Girl, stop playing." She knew how I hated to be teased.

Rachel deep throated me and it was on. We explored several positions including me power drilling her between her big titties. I was hitting it from the back and she was taking every stroke like a soldier.

"You decent in there, cuz?" Mooch was making his way down the hall.

"Not yet man." I was getting pissed because his voice was fucking with my concentration.

"Can I help?" Susan, Rachel's friend, appeared in the living room.

I smiled and soon I was fucking and getting head from both of the freaks. They were more than happy to please me and my eight inches of dick. I was enjoying my freaky threesome when Mooch came back.

"Y'all decent yet? It's almost noon." Mooch was getting on my nerves.

"Almost cuz." I was getting pissed.

"Come in here, bruh." Marco called Mooch to his room.

Thanks Marco, I thought to myself. I was enjoying every minute of this and didn't need the interruption.

I finally finished playing with the freaks, showered and got dressed. Mooch was ready to go.

"Those chicks are wild," Mooch smiled after climbing into my suburban.

"Yeah they are," I said lighting a cigarette.

"But now onto business "I know that's real. We got some big trips coming up, that's what Boss Man was telling me."

"Did you find out the pay for these trips?"

"Yeah, Fifty grand a piece."

"Oh yeah. Three or four trips like that will take care of my family for almost a year."

"I feel you man. You planning on having some more babies?"

"Naw, but I want my family to live comfortable. I'm thinking about getting Chante an SUV because her car won't be big enough for two car seats and Isis."

"I hear you, cuz. Nothing wrong with planning ahead. My son's birthday is coming up."

"Yeah, so you feel me? What time is it?"

"Five minutes until one. You wanna go sit at one of the park benches?"

"Yeah, might as well." Getting out of the truck, I noticed my phone buzzing. It was a text from Morgan.

"What is it?" Mooch noticed the concern in my face.

"Morgan just sent me a text."

"Damn. Well, you better hurry up and check it before her daddy gets here."

The text said: 'Can't wait to see you.'

"What did it say?" Mooch asked.

"She said she can't wait to see me. I wonder what she's talking about."

"We can figure that out later. Here comes her daddy."

Big Earl was riding in his black on black Hummer. He pulled up next to my ride. Mooch and I walked to either side of the Hummer and got in the back seats.

"Good afternoon gentlemen," Big Earl pulled out his Cuban cigar from the passenger seat.

"What's good?" We said in unison.

"How have my two best workers been doing?"

"I'm ok, ready to get this paper." Mooch smiled.

"Me too," I agreed.

"Yeah, congrats on the baby, Yung." Big Earl said.

"Thanks, I got another one coming too."

"What? You must be hell on these ladies."

"Not like that, it's the same chick."

"Damn boy. You gotta give her time to heal. She must have some grade A."

"That's what everyone keeps saying I will keep that in mind the next time." I was a little pissed by the comment.

"How many kids do you have, Mooch?"

"I got two. My daughter is seven and my son is three. They are by my chick in Ohio." Mooch grinned.

"That's good; we all need money for one reason or another. This new deal will guarantee you two about $200,000 a piece for four trips." Big Earl looked out of his window.

"That's right on time." I clapped and nodded at Mooch.

"Yeah man, just what I needed." Mooch agreed

"So when are we going to go on the first trip?" I asked.

"What's a good time?" Big Earl looked at both of us.

"It really doesn't matter to me," Mooch smiled.

"What about you, Yung?" Earl took a pull from his cigar.

"It depends; I got to make sure my family will be ok."

"Well, you two let me know within a week. I want to get this started as soon as possible."

"Alright, I'll give you a call in a couple of days."

"Ok, Hope to hear from you soon." Big Earl said.

We got out of the Hummer and made our way back to my truck.

"Cuz, I'm ready to make this paper. When do you think you can get away?"

I shook my head because I thought about Morgan.

"It just depends; I really don't want to be away from my baby that long."

"Did you want to miss this trip? I could probably handle it on my own."

"Naw, I need this money."

Chapter Sixteen

"Yung," Chante yelled. I was deep in thought about making that trip with Mooch.

"Whassup baby?" I responded.

"You didn't hear anything I said, did you?" She smiled and shook her head.

"I'm sorry Babe. What were you saying?"

"I was asking you what you wanted to eat tonight."

I smiled as I eased my way to my love and gently kissed her on the cheek.

"It doesn't matter to me. Whatever you decide to cook is fine because I know it's gonna be great."

"Uh huh, well since you're in such a good mood, would you mind checking on the baby. She should be waking up from her nap in a few"

"No problem."

I walked down the hallway and opened Victoria's bedroom door. My little princess was still laying on her side, fast asleep. I made my way back to the living room and fired up a cigarette. Chante made her way to the kitchen.

"I better get started on my dinner before she wakes up,"

"Don't worry baby, I will get her when she wakes up. How was your day?"

"Why are you in such a good mood today?" Chante raised her eyebrow.

"What do you mean?"

"I'm just saying."

"No reason, I can't be happy?" I lied.

"I didn't mean it like that."

Truth be told, I was far from happy but I decided to put up a happy front. I didn't want Chante to know how scared I was about making the trip. I didn't feel safe under the same roof with Morgan. She's trying to break up my happy home and I couldn't allow that to happen. I wouldn't allow that to happen. But what were my options? I couldn't just pass up on that money because I had a family to feed.

"Yung, where have you been all day?" Isis smiled as she greeted me with a hug. "

"Nowhere special sweetheart, I was just hanging out with my cousin."

Isis turned on the TV and found the Disney channel.

"Well, my sister has been bad all day."

"Really?" I laughed.

"Yes." She put her hands on her hips.

"She was in my room trying to chew on my coloring books. I told her three times to stop and then she started crying."

"Well, she is just a baby. I'm sure she didn't mean to mess up your coloring books."

"I guess not, I was trying to draw a picture for her and she just grabbed it and tried to eat it."

"That's what babies do, I'm sure you did the same thing when you were a baby."

"I don't know but I guess my next baby sister or brother will do it too. I think I'll just keep them out of my room until they get older."

I laughed, that little girl was too grown for me. I heard Victoria crying so I went into her bedroom. She started laughing as soon as she saw my face.

"What's my Lady Bug doing?" I made some silly faces and she continued smiling and she tried to sit up in her crib. "Smells like you made a stink in your diaper."

"Hello little sister, eww, she stinks."

"Yes she does," I laughed as Isis ran out of the room.

I picked up my bundle of joy and changed her soiled diaper. We made our way to the living room and I felt my phone vibrating in my pocket. "Daddy's gonna put you in your playpen and bring you a bottle."

I made my way into the kitchen; Chante was making meatloaf and listening to the radio.

"Is the baby up?"

"Yes, she dropped a dirty load and I was just coming in here to get her a bottle. It really smells good in here."

"Thanks." Chante smiled as she continued to bob her head to the music playing on the radio.

I prepared the bottle and handed it to her as she sat up in her playpen. I felt my pocket vibrate again and headed into the bathroom to check my messages. It was Morgan.

'Sup?' I wrote in my text.

'Can't wait to get you all to myself' she replied.

'Chill out. I can't talk right now.'

"Hit me up later," she responded.

I sat on the toilet with my head in my hands. I was really feeling uneasy about this upcoming trip. I needed to talk to someone. I wondered if Shannon was available to talk. I exited the bathroom and made my way to the living room. Isis and Mani were laughing and playing with each other. I decided to give my sister a call.

"Whassup bruh?" Shannon replied.

"Hey sis, are you busy right now?"

"Not really. Why?"

"I really need to holla at you," I almost whispered.

"When did you wanna talk? I can come by in an hour or so."

"Sounds good, Chante is cooking right now."

143

"That definitely sounds good and tell her to save me a plate," she laughed.

"I will. See you in about an hour."

"Alright bruh, lata."

I hung up the phone feeling a little better. If there was one person that I truly trusted, it would have to be Shannon. Talking to her would really help ease my mind. She would probably try to talk me out of the whole situation. The more and more I thought about it, I probably didn't need to go but what choices did I have?

"Babe!" Chante yelled

I got up and made my way into the kitchen.

"What's wrong?" I replied.

"I was telling you to bring the girls in the kitchen so we can get ready to eat. What's wrong with you? You have been acting funny all day." Chante frowned.

"It's really nothing Babe. I got another trip to make and I really don't want to leave you and the girls. You are pregnant again and I am really worried about you." I wrapped my arms around her.

"Aww, I will be ok.. I'm sure I can count on your family or mine if anything should happen. How long will you have to be gone?"

"Probably about four days, but I will have to go back and forth a couple of times."

"Oh." She pouted her bottom lip

"I wouldn't be doing this but it's a good investment for our family. I'm looking at making at least $200,000 on this job and we could be straight for a while off of that."

"I understand. I will just miss you." She kissed me on the cheek.

"And you know I will miss you and the girls." I embraced her.

144

"Well, it seems like you have made up your mind about things. Have a seat and I will fix you a plate in a minute."

"Shannon will be over here in a minute. She wanted you to save her a plate

"No problem."

***

Shannon made her grand entrance halfway thru dinner. I knew she would come quickly because I had mentioned Chante was cooking. She made her a plate and joined us at the table. I was happy she was here. Shannon was good with the girls. She loved them and they loved her.

"Thanks for the great meal Chante," Shannon said rubbing her full stomach.

Chante smiled as she started to clear the dinner table.

"Anytime," she said

"I can do that, you go ahead and rest. I'll do the dishes and take out the garbage."

"I'm feeling a little tired."

"You wanna lay down and watch cartoons mommy?" Isis smiled.

"Ok sweetie," Chante made her way down the hall with Isis holding her hand.

"So whassup bruh?" Shannon whispered as she helped me straighten up the kitchen.

I checked in on the baby as she play in her playpen and saw she was happy then eased to the master bedroom and saw Isis and Chante on the bed. Once I saw that my girls were set, I made my way back to the kitchen to talk to my sister.

"So what's with all the whispering?" Shannon stood with her hands on her hips.

"I got to take a job in about a week or so."

145

"Ok, what's the big deal?" she said looking confused.

"I have to go to Morgan's spot. That's where the business is supposed to take place and I have to be there four or five days at a time."

"You already know how I feel about that chick. She is bad news and you know why." She rolled her eyes

"I know sis, but what can I do? I need this money. Besides, if I don't show up the boss is gonna want to know why."

"Doesn't Earl know that you have a family now? It's not like it was in the beginning. You have a woman that's pregnant and another baby to think about."

"Yes he knows." I sighed.

"So I don't understand the problem. Just tell him that you cannot go because of your family. I'm sure there will be other jobs. Are you low on money or something?"

"I'm good but I just want to stay ahead. I have never backed down from a job before and I don't want Earl to think differently about me. I really want to get out of the game. Having a family has really changed me. I don't want to put my life or their lives in danger. It was okay when I was alone because I could take my losses as a man. But I won't risk my girls."

Shannon sat down at the kitchen table.

"Okay, if you feel this way about it, maybe you can convince Earl to let Mooch and one of his homeboys do the job."

"Yeah right, most niggas ain't ready for a big job like this. Earl would never go for that."

"Well, what are you going to do?"

"I don't know sis, I was hoping you could help me figure this out."

"Well, if you are asking me, I wouldn't go on this job. Morgan is very sneaky and I just don't trust her. She has never gotten over the fact that she had to have an abortion and you now have a family of your own. I think she's out to get you and that's why I told you to leave her alone."

"I know what you're saying sis, I just figured if I stayed cool with her everything would play itself out. I thought that if I cut her off things would really get ugly."

"But look at how things are now. Morgan has you exactly where she wants you. You work for her dad, who is a powerful man, and you are still sleeping with her. If you leave her alone, it could be bad. And if you go on the trip, it could be bad." Shannon had a point. "I really don't know what to tell you."

"I was thinking that maybe I could go on this trip but not on the next one. I will try to come up with some reason not to go. That way Earl won't be so suspicious and Morgan would get to see me." I was trying to convince myself that this was a good idea.

"I just don't know bruh," Shannon looked worried. "Have you talked to Mooch about this?"

"Yea and he pretty much feels the way you feel about it. He told me to leave her alone a long time ago but I wouldn't listen. I think I will go on this trip but miss the next one."

"I guess you don't have much choice. I'm surprised Morgan hasn't called or texted you about the trip."

"She has." I held up my phone and showed Shannon the texts.

"See, this is what I'm talking about. I wouldn't go if I was you. If you have enough money, just be done with it. You don't have any felonies so you could get a real job or go to college or something." Shannon rose to her feet.

"Are you serious?" I never gave those ideas much thought.

"Why do you sound so surprised? Believe it or not, you can make good money the legit way. It may not come as easily but at least you won't have to look over your shoulder every five minutes."

"I hear you sis, I didn't mean to make you upset. I have just never thought about what I would take up in school. All I know how to do is hustle."

"I'm sure you can find something else to do, bruh." Shannon always had a way of making a mountain look like a mole hill.

"That's easy for you to say, college girl."

"You graduated from high school bruh and last I checked you're not a dummy."

"I know, Chante would be happy about that. I think she would stop worrying about my work if she knew I was in town at a college or a real job." I was really considering going to school for a split second

"I could take you to my school if you wanted to check out some programs or talk to one of the student advisors."

"Ok sis, I'm just thinking about it. I didn't say I was definite about going or anything."

"Where are you going?" It was Chante.

"I was just suggesting that my brother go to college. I told him I would take him on campus if he was interested."

"Really?" That's great Babe. I would love for you to go legit and maybe I wouldn't have to worry about you so much."

Shannon looked at me with the 'I told you so' face.

"It's just something I have really been thinking about lately. I don't want you to worry about me because that's not good for you or the baby."

"It's definitely not. Maybe we can go on campus next week or something." Shannon said.

"Maybe." I saw how happy Chante was and I didn't want to ruin that. I wanted to make her and my babies happy. They meant the world to me and I would hate to lose them over Morgan and her bullshit.

Chapter Seventeen

I decided to talk to Mooch about my plans for this next job. I didn't want to miss out on any money but I couldn't risk losing my family.

I loved Saturday afternoons with my family. Chante spent her mornings in bed. She was over her morning sickness and into her second trimester. My baby definitely had her mood swings and food cravings but I didn't mind. She was having a boy and I'm excited. At first, the doctors thought it was a girl but apparently he had been sitting with his legs crossed.

I decided to let Chante get some rest so I took the girls to my mom's house for a couple hours. Morgan had been texting me all day but I decided to ignore her completely. I knew there was a chance that she could say something to her dad but maybe she wouldn't if she thought I was still coming to see her. I'm really not sure but that's just gonna have to be the chance that I take.

Mooch was calling.

"Sup fam?" I replied.

"I was just checking on you. What time you coming by?"

"I'm on the way right now. I just dropped the girls off at my mom's so Chante can get some rest."

"Alright fam. I'm at the house."

It felt good to be in the old neighborhood. It reminded me of my carefree days and how reckless I had been in my life. I had met, pimped and slept with a lot of women from this neighborhood. Chicks had never really meant shit to me. Easy come and easy go. Morgan and Chante had really been my only exceptions. Two out a one hundred was pretty bad. I never thought about consequences or things that could happen; I just did what I wanted to do. Chante entered my life and now I saw things differently. I fucked with a lot of bitches but they always knew their place. I know I should have cut everyone off but I just couldn't. I just prayed that my ways didn't cause me to lose the love of my life.

I pulled up to Mooch's apartment and just sat in my truck for a few minutes. I went through my phone, reading all the texts from Morgan that day. That girl definitely had something up her sleeve. I hated to admit it but I was truly scared; scared of what could happen. I was afraid that Morgan would confront my woman and that my woman would take my kids away. I had a son on the way; a future 'Yung' and I wanted to be there for him. I didn't want to lose my family because I was unable to let go of my past. I needed to break free from Morgan. The rest of the hoes were never a problem but Morgan was a definite threat. I had been putting this off for way too long. I had to think of a way to get her out of my life completely without hurting Chante in the process.

I was startled by Mooch knocking on the window. I snapped out of my thoughts and got out of the car.

"Are you ok, fam?" Mooch looked a little concerned.

"No, not really."

Mooch looked around at the neighbors. "This place has been hot for the past couple of days so let's go inside."

We made our way in the house and I sat on the couch. Mooch went into the kitchen and came back with a six pack of Bud Light.

"So what's going on around here?" I popped the top off of a beer and took a nice gulp.

"Man, you know Darlene from across the street?"

151

"Yeah," I replied.

"Well, her man caught her cheating with Trent from down the block."

"What? I thought he messed with her sister?"

Mooch laughed. "He does. They were at her crib shootin' the other night. The cop was over there twice."

"Damn." I smiled but on the inside I felt sorry for Darlene. Her tragedy could become my tragedy if I don't get Morgan out of my life.

"So what's going on with you?" Mooch asked.

I finished the first beer and immediately popped the top on the next one.

"Cuz, I should have listened to you from the very beginning. I never should have started things back up with Morgan. I don't know what I was thinking. I got to find a way to get this chick out of my life and for good this time. I got too much at stake and I'm not trying to lose my family."

"I feel ya, I'm not gonna hit you with an 'I told you so' but I think I might have a way to solve your problem."

"What is it?" I was so excited.

"Maybe we can take Marco along on the trip. Just hear me out before you say no. Morgan doesn't know my brother so we can say he is just a friend of ours. If you miss a trip or two, Marco can go in your place. Maybe he can flirt with Morgan a little bit, make it seem like you and him aren't really close. He could tell her that if anything happened between them; it would stay between them. You feel me?"

"So, we could get Marco to start sexing her and somehow have proof of it. I can make like I am so disappointed in her and maybe she will chill out.

152

What if she threatens to go to her dad about our past?"

"That's simple. We will just show the evidence to Earl. Let him see his daughter in error, sleeping and flirting with his business associates. He will be so mad that he won't listen to what she's saying. Where is her proof? Does she have any pictures of you with her? Any letters or anything showing that the two of you messed around?"

"Nothing other than texts in her phone. We gotta get Marco to delete anything from her phone that ties me to her. I never wrote any letters or took pictures with her. If she has a picture of me, it's from seeing me in the hood or something. Nothing naked or anything like that."

"Ok, so we know what we need to do. I will talk to Marco tomorrow and let him know what's up. Me and you will go on this run and the next time, Marco can go in your place. Stop worrying so much, you know I got your back."

"No doubt." I nodded and breathed a little easier. Mooch did have a fool-proof plan. Marco loved the ladies just as much as we did, so talking to Morgan shouldn't be a problem. I can't believe that I didn't think of that myself.

"So how long are you going to chill?" Mooch looked down at his phone.

"I guess I can stay awhile but I just need to call and check on Chante. She is at home resting and I took the girls over to my momma's house."

"Aiight, well, go ahead and do that. I will be right back."

Mooch went to his room and I decided to give Chante a call. She sounded like she was asleep. I figured she would be okay for a little while but I

153

didn't want to stay out too late. I knew the girls were comfortable at mommas so I decided to unwind and drink another beer. Mooch soon emerged from his room.

"Yeah...that's whassup," Mooch hung up the phone and walked into the kitchen.

"What you got going?" I asked.

"You know me; I got some stress-relievers on their way over here. I figured you could use some of that."

"You wild," I laughed.

Minutes later there was a knock on the door.

"Right on time," Mooch said and opened the door.

"Hello boys," It was Kelsey and Karen; two suburban white chicks that we fucked with every now and then.

"How you been ladies?"

"Definitely been missing you, Yung," Kelsey smiled and winked.

"Oh yeah, you gonna show me how much you missed me?"

"Well, I guess that's our cue to exit." Mooch smiled and grabbed Karen's hand.

They made their way to Mooch's room. I heard him shut the door and blast the volume on the stereo.

Kelsey began to take off her blouse. She was wearing a sheer black bra that accentuated her double D breasts. They looked so inviting and her nipples were hard.

"Yes, I will show you how much I missed you, Yung."

She made her way over to the couch where Kelsey was and she quickly unfastened my pants and started massaging my dick.

"Stop playing with that, Kelsey," I moaned.

She ignored my demands and put my dick between her luscious breasts.

"Oh shit," I moaned.

She placed me in her mouth and began massaging me with her tongue. I could feel my body grow weaker.

"Put it inside me," she breathed.

I flipped her over and gave her my best action. Kelsey loved it in her ass. I played in her pussy while I felt myself nut. This girl had some grade A pussy. We took turns pleasing each other orally. I drove Kelsey crazy with my tongue action and she drove me crazy with hers. We ended with me releasing my load deep in her throat.

"Damn girl, I needed that." I smacked her on ass.

"Glad I could help," She laughed.

"You did that," I smiled.

"So, what are y'all doing tonight?" She straightened herself up and headed for the bathroom. I decided to join her.

"Nothing," I replied.

We each found a towel and wash cloth and then bathed.

"Karen and I were trying to find something to do for the night." Kelsey said applying some lip gloss to her pouty lips.

"Well, I gotta check on my girl but maybe I can stay her for a while." I quickly sent Chante a text.

"Too bad you can't stay the night," Kelsey winked.

"Definitely not, but I can stay until midnight at least."

I figured I would call my mom and see if the girls could spend the night. I knew she wouldn't mind and by the time I got home, Chante would probably be in bed. I would just keep checking on her and that should be ok.

***

I finished freshening up and then called Momma. She said the girls could spend the night. Mani would probably stay up half the night. Chante spent most of her time in bed. Our son was really taking a toll on her body. She often said how she never had those problems with the girls.

"So whassup?" Mooch and Karen made their way into the living room.

"Are y'all gonna kick it for a little while or what?"

All eyes were on me; mainly because I was the only one in a relationship and with a slight curfew.

"I guess I can stay for a little while," I nodded.

"That's good," Mooch smiled as he and Karen made their way to the loveseat.

"So, what do you guys want to do?"

"What's on your mind, Miss?" I grinned.

"Let's play a game," She winked at Karen.

"What?" Mooch and I said in unison.

"C'mon you guys, live a little bit. Step outside of the box. It's something different and it's fun."

"Is there any sex involved?" Mooch asked.

"Possibly, so are you game or lame?"

"What kind of game is it?" I asked.

I'm not really into all the games and shit. I do realize these are white chicks and white chicks are the freakiest. They get into the entire role playing and that's not what I'm into.

"It's a drinking game, basically someone makes a statement and if you have ever been in that situation, you take a drink. Ok, for example, I might say 'been in a threesome'...if you have been in a threesome, you take a drink,"

156

"Ok, sounds kinda stupid to me," Mooch replied.

"Well, don't knock it until you try it." Kelsey said

"Ok, so who starts?" I asked.

"I will. But first someone needs to get the liquor." Kelsey said to Mooch.

Mooch went into the kitchen and brought back a fifth of Remy Martin.

"Well, I think that will definitely get the party started."

"I won't be partying long because I still have to go home. I hope I don't end up taking too many shots."

***

At 2:00 a.m., we were all laughing so hard that we were in tears. I guess that drinking game was more fun after seven or eight shots.

I looked at my phone. I had three missed calls from Chante.

"Damn. I gotta make a phone call." I went into kitchen and dialed Chante's number.

She only let it ring once. She immediately fired off on me.

"What the hell is going on, Yung? Where are my girls and where in the hell are you?" She yelled.

"I am so sorry babe. The girls are at my mom's house. I figured you could use the rest and momma wanted them to stay. She said she was going to take them shopping tomorrow. I am still at Mooch's house with a couple friends. We been playing cards, listening to music and drinking."

"I can definitely tell that you have been drinking and I'm glad to know that everyone is okay. I really didn't know what to think. I woke up and no one was here."

"I know. I'm sorry I didn't hear my phone the first time you called." I could hear my voice dragging on every word

"Well I'm ok now, just send me a text or a voicemail the next time you decide to stay out with the girls."

"I will babe," I smiled.

"And don't worry about driving home right now. You are at your cousin's house so just sleep it off over there. I don't want you to risk getting pulled over for a DUI or something."

"Ok babe," I was surprised.

"Cuz," Can you hand me another beer out of the fridge?" Mooch yelled as he entered the kitchen.

"You tell Mooch to slow his roll over there."

"Hey cuz, Chante said for you to slow your roll."

"It's ok Chante; I'm taking the next few drinks for you."

"I guess you heard him babe, glad that Mooch had come into the kitchen. If Chante had doubted my whereabouts, Mooch had just confirmed it.

"Well tell him to drink a fifth of vodka for me, try not to make yourself sick babe. I will see you when you get home. I'm going over to your mom's today. So don't worry about picking up the girls; I will get them."

"Ok Bae, I love you."

"Love you too," she replied as she hung up the phone.

I had such a remarkable and understanding woman. Although the liquor had the best of me, I could not forget the wonderful woman I had at home. She never doubts me and we hardly ever fight. Mooch and Shannon are right, I do have everything I need at home. I need to stop playing the field and focus on my family before one of these jump-offs cause me to lose everything.

Chapter Eighteen

I had been trying not to think about the trip to Morgan's. Unfortunately, the day had finally come. I can't help but wonder how this trip will play out and how I will ever rid myself of Morgan. Even with Mooch's plan in place, I wasn't so sure that it would work. It was too late to turn back because Mooch and I were officially on the road. You could cut the tension with a knife; I had not said a word for over an hour.

"Cuz, what are you thinking about over there? I have been trying to talk to you for the past twenty minutes. I thought you were listening but now I'm just gonna assume that you was only bobbin' your head to the music all this time."

"I'm sorry fam, I was over here in my own little world. Whassup?"

"What's on your mind?"

"You already know."

"You're still worrying about that? I told you not to worry. I made a call to Earl before we hit the road. I told him that your girl was having complications with this pregnancy and that you are really worried about leaving her days at a time. I told him I had a partner that would be filling in for you a couple times. Earl trusts me, so he knows I wouldn't bring any loose niggas into his business. So as far as Earl and Morgan know, Marco is a friend of mine that will be covering for you. I never mentioned that we are related and I never mentioned that you and Marco know one another. I had been doing dirt with other dudes before I brought you into the organization so it's not a surprise to Earl. Cuz, I told you, I got your back. So try not to worry and let's get this money."

"I'm doing the best I can fam. I guess I was just thinking about the worst case scenario. I don't want to lose my family. The game was much easier in the beginning because in the beginning I only had to worry about myself. Chante came into my life and changed the game. I know that I have been doing wrong but I promise, if I can make my way out of this without Chante finding out, I'm finished playing around for good. I have never said those words before but Chante and the girls are all I need."

"Gotta be real love, I have never heard you say anything about putting your player ways behind you. That's good and I hope I can find a woman that makes me feel the same way. I been thinking, women get mad when niggas play the field but the only reason we play is because we are waiting on that right woman to make us stop."

"Really cuz? Normally I would agree with you but that's not my answer anymore. Chante has always been a good woman but I continued to play the game. She never did anything but love me but look at how the game has turned on me. We can't put the blame on the women anymore; we do what we want to do because we are men. It doesn't matter how good or pure our women are, if we want to play, we will. Being a man, we just blame the woman to protect our pride. What man wants to look stupid?"

"I guess so, I never really thought about it like that." Mooch didn't like hearing the truth when it came to him and his ways.

Ring Ring

"Hello." It was Morgan.

"Hey sexy, how close are you guys to my house?"

"We still got a ways to go." I was still trying to prepare myself for the next couple of days.

161

"Probably be there in two to two and a half hours."

"Oh ok, I'm so looking forward to you."

"I bet." I replied.

"I did want to talk to you about something though."

"Oh yea, whassup?" I felt a lump in my throat.

"My dad said your chick was having problems with her pregnancy. I just wanted to say that I was sorry to hear that. And who is Mooch's friend, some guy named Marco?"

I smiled because our plan was already working.

"Thank you for your concern for the baby. As for Mooch's friend, you might want to talk to him about that because I don't really know him. I have seen him once or twice but can't tell you much about him."

"Oh. So, he is not a friend of yours?"

"Naw, me and Mooch are family but I'm not the only person he hangs with. Did you wanna talk to him?"

"Naw, I will just talk to you guys when you get here."

"Aiight, shawty." I hung up.

"What was that all about?" Mooch looked puzzled.

"The first phase of our plan is working Cuz, Morgan called."

"Oh yea, and what was she saying?"

"She was asking questions about your friend Marco. She wanted to know if we were friends and of course I told her no."

"See Cuz, I told you that Earl and Morgan would believe my story. This isn't the first time I have brought some of my homeboys into a job. I just stopped recruiting new faces when you decided to come on board."

"I'm so glad, I really think she bought the whole thing. I'm glad they have never seen me with Marco and that I have never mentioned him."

"Yep, I told you things are going to work out. You just make sure you really leave Morgan alone after this. Marco knows what to do because I already talked to him. Little brother feels so honored that we are involving him, so I know he won't slip up or let us down."

"You're right. So far everything is looking up. I just got to get through these couple of days and pray that nothing goes wrong."

"You are the master. You got Morgan wide open. Keep her that way while we are up here. Make her feel like she is so important, it will only make her fucking with Marco more painful."

"You right. You are absolutely right."

***

Mooch and I arrived at Morgan's apartment around 11:30 a.m. I had already talked to Chante before we pulled up in Morgan's apartment complex. That phone call ought to tide her over for a couple hours. The Wandering Hills apartments were your typical luxury apartments. I could tell from the gold and white gates at the entrance of the complex; these apartments were definitely for the upper class. The average rent for a one bedroom probably ran from $950 .00 to $1,000 a month. Nothing, but the very best for Earl's baby girl; the girl that was potentially crippling me.

"What's the apartment number?" Mooch asked as he turned down his stereo. Mooch's old-school car felt out of place with all the BMW's, Porches', and other luxury cars.

"We are looking for apartment 143B," I replied. I looked in awe as we passed a recreation area, Olympic sized outdoor pool and a fully-equipped weight room.

"Damn, I wouldn't mind staying in a place like this. You know the police rarely ride around up here. If they do, it's probably because they live here."

"Yea, it definitely looks legit. I can see why Earl wanted us to post up here. This would be the last place the cops would suspect any dope dealings. I give Earl a lot of credit; he really knows how to maintain his business. A lot of guys keep getting ratted out back home because they are too obvious about their set up. Never set up shop in the hood but them small time boys will never learn."

"I agree with you on that Cuz, I'm glad we are working for a man with a good head on his shoulders. There's something I have wanted to ask you about."

"And what is that?" I questioned.

"Since you really plan on ending things with Morgan, Are you still going to be able to do business with Earl?"

"Naw, I love the money but I know that things will never be the same. If I cut Morgan off, I will have to sever all ties with Earl too. It just wouldn't be safe. I think I'm gonna call my sister, Amari, and find out the prices of houses out where she lives."

"You just gonna leave?" Mooch looked shocked

"Cuz, you know I would have to move. Morgan would be hounding me and Earl would try to talk me back into working for him. No one knows where Amari lives except for family. So I know for sure that we would be safe."

164

"Ok, but how are you going to convince Chante to move? You just gonna tell her that y'all are moving without any explanation?"

"I see what you are saying. I guess I didn't think about that. I will find a way to convince her. I will talk to my sister and try to convince Chante that moving is for the best."

"Well good luck with that."

"Yeah, I know."

The plan was for us to just look like some typical college students. We were not dressed fancy in our typical swag. Instead, we tried to blend in with the surrounding culture. We grabbed our book bags out of trunk and headed for the door.

"You probably don't want to hear this, but I bet there are some freaks in these apartments."

"You're right cuz, due to my already fucked up situation, I definitely didn't want to hear that. But if we come across some."

"I already know fam," Mooch gave me some dap and I knocked on Morgan's apartment door.

"Hello," Morgan wrapped her arms around my neck as I tried to make my way into her place.

"I thought you guys would never get here."

"Ok Morgan, let my man get in the front door before you jump on him."

"I was trying, he knows how long I have been trying to get him to come visit me. I'm gonna be so happy for the next couple of days."

"I bet." Mooch said and winked.

"I hope y'all are done playing. Business before pleasure."

"I hear ya, I'm going to call the connect so we can get past the business and go to the pleasure part of this trip." Morgan nibbled on my neck.

Morgan gave me one last look and headed to her bedroom with my book bag.

"Oh yeah, I feel for you cuz."

Chapter Nineteen

I can't say that I had been getting much sleep since arriving at Morgan's but cash flow was been lovely. The more time I spent with Morgan, the more relaxed and laid back she got. I had been able to talk to Chante without any problems or objections from Morgan. I figured she was cool because I was there with her. Chante had called to tell me that her doctor recommended she go on maternity leave as soon as possible. Our son was causing a lot of fluid build-up in her body and she needed to stay off her feet as much as possible. I wasn't stressed about her losing income because I had managed to save over $250,000. We ought to be able to find somewhere to live with over a quarter of a million dollars.

"Yung," Morgan whined as she came in the bathroom. I had just made it out of the shower.

"Morg." I teased her.

"Do you and Mooch wanna go to this party tomorrow night?"

"Did someone say a party?" I heard Mooch from the living room.

"I dunno but ask Cuz, girl let me put some clothes on."

"But you know I like you better without your clothes on." Morgan whined.

"Get out of here you little freak," I said and smacked her on the ass. She walked into the living room with Mooch. I wasn't feeling the party scene. I didn't want anyone to see me with Morgan. It could come back to bite me in the ass later.

"Hurry up Cuz," Mooch yelled up the hall.

"Man don't rush me," I joked. I enjoyed taking my time. My clothes were pressed. Regardless of where I was, I was always fly. No one would ever say I looked a mess in these streets. I finished dressing and made my way to the living room.

"So whassup? You going to the party or not?"

"Naw I'm good." I could see immediately that both of them were very disappointed with my answer.

"Why don't you want to go?" Morgan said snapping her neck.

"Don't get mad at me Morg; I'm just tryna chill and get this paper. You and Mooch can go to the party. You can introduce Mooch to some of your friends and I will be here in case a money call comes through."

"But I wanted you to go with me," she was whining again.

"But you know I will be here when you get back. Go ahead and shake your ass at the party because you know I'm gonna put it down when you get home."

"Oh, Is that right?" Morgan smiled.

Morgan climbed on my lap and started kissing me passionately. I started massaging her breast and she was reaching for my dick.

"Excuse me; did y'all forget that I was in here?" Mooch asked.

"My bad Mooch, I guess you will be my date tonight."

"That's whassup. I been wanting to cut something since I got here. Try to find me a freak." Mooch face lit up.

"I will introduce you to some of my friends, but you will have to find out the freaky part on your own."

"So, when am I gonna find out your freaky part?" I glanced over at her. I knew how to play Morgan. All I had to do was give her the dick and she would do whatever I say. Dick works just like bait to these thirsty hoes. I kinda feel bad saying hoe with Morgan but I guess she was my hoe.

"Step into this room and you can find out right now."

***

I thought that I might have a lower sperm count because Morgan had sucked me dry. I came in her mouth twice before I had to make her stop. Morgan was a beast with that head. I couldn't lie, she was so much better than Chante but I would never tell her that. I was glad I'd gotten that problem out of the way and they were getting ready to leave out for the party. I was sure that would give me a good four to five hours without her hanging on my every move. I was glad Mooch was going. He would let me know when they were on the way back; just in case.

"You sure you don't want to go with us?" Mooch asked.

"I'm sure Cuz but y'all have a good time. I'm just gonna wait for any money calls and probably get something to eat a little later."

"I'm gonna miss you Yung," Morgan pouted as she grabbed her purse.

I looked her over. Morgan was wearing a red mini dress that showed all her curves. She was wearing her hair and curly. "Well, you will definitely turn some heads with that dress on."

"Do you like it babe?" She modeled for me.

"I'm gonna love taking it off of you later," I grabbed her butt before they made it out the door.

I walked outside and sat on the terrace as they drove away. Mooch said he would call me when they were headed home and I hoped he didn't bring any chicks to the crib. He had money to get a hotel room

169

and I didn't want all any chicks here knowing my face. A sexy little redhead waved at me from next door. I nodded at her. I saw her checking me out yesterday when Morgan and I were making a run.

"I'm sorry if I am being too bold. My name is Alicia." Ms. Redhead made her way to the porch and sat down beside me.

"I'm Yung. Nice to meet you miss."

"Did you just move in here with your girlfriend?" Alicia was a little nosey.

"No Shawty, me and my friend are just students and friends of Morgan's."

"Oh, I guess I assumed wrong."

"It's ok, I'm a longtime friend of Morgan's and I would rather people think I'm her man. It keeps a lot of the crazy guys away."

"I guess I see your point. I guess you could be rather intimidating."

"Oh yeah? I guess I don't intimidate you."

"No, not at all. I am glad that wasn't your girlfriend."

"And why is that?" I tried to act surprised.

"Because, I'm not a home wrecker." Alicia eased her way closer to me. It was dark and no one was outside but the two of us.

"Well, I guess that's good to know." I pulled her a little closer and placed her hand on my throbbing dick.

"Oh my," she giggled.

"What's wrong boo, He won't bite and no one is around.? Why don't you kiss on it a little bit?" I said pulling out my python

I didn't have to ask her twice. Alicia's head was bobbing while I tried to pay attention for any unwanted audiences. Just as I was really getting into it, my phone began to ring.

"Are you going to answer that?" Alicia paused but continued licking on the head of my dick. It was Morgan.

"Yea, I will try, but don't you stop what you are doing."

"Ok," she slurped away.

"Hello," I breathed.

"Hey Boo I just wanted to let you know that we made it to the party safely." Morgan yelled trying to talk over the music in the background.

"Oh, well that's good." I groaned as I tried to keep from nutting. I didn't want this feeling to be over.

"What are you doing?"

"Nothing, just sitting on the porch and relaxing,"

"Alright boo, I will see you later."

"See you later." I couldn't wait to hang up the phone. Alicia had my toes curling. I felt like I was going to jump off the porch from the pleasure.

"Damn girl, you are about to make me nut and you better catch it all."

Alicia just continued to nod as I watched her deep throat my dick. I felt my juices squirt out and she swallowed it all.

"So, how was it?" She licked her lips

"Why don't you invite me to your place and I will show you."

I fastened my pants and we walked into Alicia's apartment. I can't say that I paid much attention to her décor because I wanted her body. She stripped down to nothing and lay back on the bed. She massaged her clit and then tasted her juices.

"Can I have a taste?" I gently kissed her lips and sucked on her tongue while squeezing her nipples.

171

She moaned.

I made my way past her naval ring and licked her inner thigh.

"Don't tease me," She whined.

I spread her clean shaven pussy lips and sucked on her clit. She moaned so loud that I had to put her panties in her mouth. Alicia was a squirter and that shit turned me on. I made her come twice and she let me fuck her in her ass. She was really into the anal sex. That was cool with me because I wasn't trying to make any more babies. She sucked me off once more and then we said our good-byes. It was nice to make a new friend; a bitch to fuck when Morgan went to class.

I decided to text Mooch and see what time they would be home. He said they might go to an afterhours spot but he would let me know for sure. I told him to talk Morgan into that. I could spend more time with my new freak who already wanted to suck on me again. I knew I was in the wrong but I figured I might as well enjoy all this while I still could. After I finished up this business, I planned on retiring from the game.

***

I woke up to the sound of my ringing phone. It was Mooch.

"Whassup Fam?" I said dazed.

"Damn old man," Mooch laughed. I could hear laughter in the background

"Don't tell me that you are already in bed for the night."

"Man, shut up." I looked around and noticed I had passed out on the couch.

"Whassup and what time is it?

"We still at the party but we are definitely hitting up the afterhours joint." Mooch was obviously drunk.

"Ok, that's good to know."

"Yea, it's almost 1 a.m. and the after hour's spot jumps from two until whenever."

"Ok," I sat up on the couch and looked around for my cigarettes.

"Morgan is drinking and having a good time. I told her to let me know when she was ready to leave the afterhours. I have already found my girlfriend for the night. She got her own crib, so I'm probably gonna crash over there. I'm still gonna call and let you know when Morgan is headed to the apartment."

"Aiight, thanks."

"No problem. Well, I gotta get back to these ladies."

"Aiight Cuz, have fun."

I hung up with Mooch and decided to check my phone. I had two texts from Morgan, a missed call from Shannon about thirty minutes ago, a goodnight text from Chante and two missed calls from Alicia. I sent Alicia a text but decided to call my sister. It rang three times before she answered.

"Whassup sis?"

"Oh nothing much.. How's your trip going?" Shannon sounded sarcastic

"See, you are always with that shit."

"Yeah whatever. But really, how is it going?"

"Good I guess."

"I'm sure Morgan is on cloud nine right about now."

"Actually, she is clubbing with Mooch and I am at the house all alone,"

"What? I thought she would be stuck to you like glue. I guess you really are the master."

"Stop it! Plus, you can stop worrying. I can promise you that once this mission is complete; I'm through with Morgan and the whole organization."

"Oh really." Shannon didn't sound convinced.

"Yes really, I called Amari and she is checking out available houses in her neighborhood. I know it's impossible for me to have a great life around Morgan; so I plan on moving my family. I have quite a bit of money saved and this run alone will get me some more dough. So you can believe me when I say that I'm done."

"I'm sorry bruh, I hear you but I just can't believe it. I'm really glad that you are finally putting your family's needs in front of your wants. What about Mooch? I'm sure he doesn't plan on getting out of the organization. Won't he need someone to replace you?"

"We have already discussed that little sister."

"Well, good for you. I pray that everything works out for you."

"Well ok sis, call me tomorrow. I'm gonna fix something to eat, burn one and probably go back to sleep." I looked at my phone and saw that Alicia had responded to my text. Figured; might as well take advantage of this neighbor while I have a couple of hours.

"You probably have some ass lined up. You better hurry before your stalker makes it home."

"I love you sis." I just smiled.

"Love you too bruh and I will call you tomorrow."

Chapter Twenty

I woke up to the smell of Belgium waffles and music playing. I yawned and looked at the clock on the wall; it was 11:30 a.m. I wondered what time Morgan made it in this morning. I hung out with the neighbor for about an hour and tapped out. I heard Mooch laughing from the kitchen; I didn't think he would be awake this early because he was so wasted the night before.

"The dead has finally arisen. You was sleeping so sound that I couldn't wake you up." Morgan giggled and greeted me with a kiss.

"I'm sorry, I guess I let that liquor get the best of me."

"Yeah, Cuz never could handle that white liquor." Mooch chuckled.

"Anyways, you missed some great parties."

"Yeah you did," Mooch chimed in as he stuffed his mouth.

"I'm glad y'all had a good time."

"I think there's gonna be another party tonight."

"Oh yeah?" I tried not to look interested or excited.

"Yeah, I'm trying to get Morgan to go with me but she acting like she wants to stay home with you all day."

"I missed you last night boo. I mean, I had a good time but I wanted to spend some time with you while you are here," Morgan said.

"We got time. Mooch likes to get out and meet people, you know that. So since he is in your town, you should take him out and show him around. I'm gonna be here, so you don't have to worry about me." I kissed her on the cheek

"Uh huh, I will think about it." she rolled her eyes.

"Well, maybe I can convince you after I use the bathroom." I nodded at Mooch and he nodded back. I had to stick to the plan and so far it was working.

I made my way to the bathroom and decided to check my phone. Chante had called twice so I decided to call her back

"Hello baby.

"Hello, I wondered when you would wake up." Chante giggled.

"Oh really?"

"Yeah, I tried calling you earlier but your phone kept going to voicemail. You must be working really long nights."

"Yea Babe, plus we been drinking a little too much. You know I can't handle a lot of liquor."

"Ain't that the truth, I can definitely drink you under the table. It's been so long since I have been able to drink. You can probably out drink me now."

"Aw, my poor baby."

"That's the problem; you keep putting babies in your baby."

"So I guess this is all my fault?" I laughed.

"Well, you definitely played a part in all this."

"How are you feeling and how are the girls?"

"I have just been sleeping a lot. Shannon has been spending the night to help with the girls. Mani has been wearing me out lately. Sometimes it strains my back having to pick her up and just keeping up with her. Isis has really been my big helper; she is such a good big sister."

"I miss you all and I will be glad when we make it back home," I sighed because I really did miss my family. That's one thing that had never changed. None of the random girls could ever compete with my love for Chante or our girls. That's how I knew

176

that our love was real because I never had to second guess it.

"We miss you too. When will you be home?"

"We should be leaving out tomorrow around noon,"

"I can't wait. So what time will you make it home?"

"If we leave around noon, we should make it home by 5pm."

"Sounds good to me. Well, I didn't want anything so just call me back later or I will call you a little later."

"Alright my love."

Talk to you later Yung, I love you."

"I love you too."

I had such a good thing going with Chante and I was really starting to feel guilty about all the hoes. What's a man to do? As I hung up with Chante, I noticed I had two text messages from Alicia. I decided to hit her up.

"Sup?" I texted.

'You and me later I hope...lol' She replied.

'Do u have any plans later?' I responded.

'Going to the gym, grocery shopping, but nothing too major.'

'Alright, I will hit u up'

Knock Knock

"I'm on the way out!" I shouted. I hate being rushed when I'm doing anything.

"Ok babe, I thought you fell in or something."

"I will be out in a minute girl." I rubbed my head at the sadness of a thirsty chic.

As I made my way to the kitchen, I heard Morgan and Mooch discussing the club scene. I hope I could convince this girl to go out again tonight. I was trying to spend little to no time with her. I also tried to keep it mostly business because it's bad enough that I was still sleeping with her. The more time I spend with Morgan, the deeper she got under my skin.

"What y'all laughin' about?" I put on a fake smile.

"Awe man, we just talking about them drunk hoes from last night. They started stripping in the club and you know I was throwing money at they ass."

"I'm sure," I nodded remembering those days. Just thinking about all the money I wasted in the strip clubs made me wanna throw up.

"They was really trippin'. One of the girls tried to give me a lap dance."

"Look at you, my boo got the chicks jockin'."

"Shut up Yung." Morgan began to blush.

"Anyways, you seemed like you was feeling the blond chick."

"Shut up Mooch, we was just drunk and having a good time. Don't try to blow the thing out of proportion."

"Don't worry Bae, if you ever wanna get down with another female, it's fine with me. I just want to watch."

"Me too," Mooch chimed in.

Morgan smiled at me and rolled her eyes at Mooch. But I was sure she would do all of the above if I asked her to do it. That really started to bother me. Why would a woman let a man have that much influence over them? I could basically tell a hoe to rob a bank and half of them would be ask 'which bank? It's sad.

"Aiight cuz, chill out." Mooch knew I could care less about him watching Morgan fuck anyone; she wasn't my main chick.

"Back to the real issue; what's up for tonight? We should go to Club Banger, some chicks was talking about it last night."

"Well you can count me out, someone has to be focused on the money at night. But y'all should go out and have a good time."

"Why don't you wanna go?" You was always the life of the party and now you just want to sit around the house." Morgan asked

"Like I said, someone has to be focused on the cash flow at night. What if some big plays come thru? We would miss out on the money if we are all wasted in the club. I doubt your dad would be happy about that. Plus, the main reason we are here is to make money, so I'm trying to be about my business."

"I hear ya, and my dad would get pissed if he missed out on any money. I just wanted us to do things together."

"Well why don't you step in this bedroom and we can find something to do together," I said leading the way.

"Sounds good to me." Morgan shut the door behind us.

I must have dozed off after round three because I woke up in a daze. I fastened my pants, went to the bathroom and washed my face. There was complete silence in the apartment so I figured Mooch and Morgan decided to make some plays without me. I checked my phone and noticed I had some missed calls and had a few messages. Chante had texted that she loved me and mentioned that the girls were okay and Alicia wanted to know when we could hook up. I had missed calls from Mooch, Morgan and Shannon. I decided to give Mooch a call first

"Bout time you woke up," Mooch was laughing and I heard music in the background.

"Whassup?" I replied.

"Me and Morg are making a couple drops on the Southside. Thought you might want to know."

"Ok that's good. When will you be back?"

"We got two more stops to make and then we going by Applebee's."

"Ok, and what about later on tonight?"

"We going out. I convinced Morgan to go with me because I don't want to sit around the house. Might as well have some fun while I'm here."

"Thanks fam, Morgan is really starting to get on my nerves. I'm glad your brother agreed to make the next trip up here. Morgan just won't take no for an answer and I'm trying to stick to the plan."

"I feel you cuz, I will call you when we make it to Applebee's in case you are still hungry."

"Aiight" I was happy. Mooch always knew what I was thinking. I didn't want Morgan popping up on me, so it was good to know their every move.

"See you later," Mooch replied.

***

I decided I would give Shannon a call since I had the crib to myself for a while.

"What's going on bruh?" Shannon questioned.

"What you mean?" I asked.

"I called you a couple hours ago."

"I'm sorry sis, I dozed off."

"You are really doing too much."

"Anyway, Is everything ok?" I cut her off

"You mean are Chante and the kids alright? Yes, they are fine. I'm kinda worried about Chante though."

"Why?"

180

"I really think this sudden pregnancy is really getting the best of her. She tries to do normal things and she just doesn't have the energy. I have basically been staying here because she really needs the help with the girls."

"Yea, she told me that you was staying and I really appreciate it."

"It's no problem but you should make her go to the doctor when you get back. I really think she needs to be off work until the baby comes, she looks ill."

"Ok, I'll definitely get her to a doctor this coming Monday. I told Chante to stop working but you know how she is."

"Yea, so independent but she really needs to rest more. Momma is driving me crazy."

"Oh no, what is it now?"

"Where do I start?" She paused.

"April is talking about moving out and momma doesn't want her to. I don't know why she wants to put up with April's drama but you know how momma is. She is still mad that Amari moved to a different state. Then she was mad that you are not at home with your family."

"I knew that was coming, I would call momma, but I know I will never get off the phone. I plan on going by her house when I get back."

"It might be safer if you call her, she went off like thirty minutes ago. She even said that you was acting like daddy because you are out and about while Chante is struggling with the kids."

"What, I know she didn't go there? I know I'm not perfect but I'm nothing like daddy. I'm out on business, I'm not just out here getting ass and making more babies. I haven't left my family for another one, so she can miss me with all that."

"Calm down bruh. You know that I know the truth but you know how momma thinks."

"Yea, but she still doesn't need to put me in the same category as daddy. I won't leave my family. I know everything that I'm doing isn't right but my family lives good and they ain't asking for nothing."

"I feel you bruh, just thought I would give you the heads up."

"I appreciate it sis, so what's new with you?" I felt better knowing my sister had my back.

"Nothing really just helping out with my sister-in-law and my nieces. I will be glad when you get back, I miss my smoking partner."

"I miss you too sis. We should be leaving out tomorrow around noon."

"When do you have to go back?"

"I was supposed to come back up here in two weeks but Marco is filling in for me,

"Marco! You goin' let our 'wildcard' cousin replace you? Are you sure that's a good idea?"

"Marco is straight and he's part of my plan to get rid of Morgan. We have already talked about it and the boss knows he is a reliable guy. You worry too much," I tried to reassure her.

"Yea ok, I guess Marco is just a younger you. Do you think Morgan will fall for his charms?" She blurted out.

"I think so. Morgan doesn't know that Marco is my cousin, so she probably won't think anything about sleeping with him. As far as everyone else knows, Marco is just one of Mooch's homeboys."

"So no one knows that him and Mooch are brothers?"

"No," I smiled at my master plan.

"Ok, that plan might work."

"It will sis," I reassured her.

Alicia was texting me again. She was truly persistent.

"Sis, I will talk to you later."

"Alright big man, take it easy."

"Love you too."

I decided to go over to Alicia's; I really didn't want her coming over here. I didn't know Alicia that well and I didn't trust her around my personal shit. I walked down the hallway, making sure no one was out or watching me as I knocked on the door.

"Come on in," Alicia sighed.

As I entered her apartment I could smell the lavender incense that she was burning. The blinds were closed and Alicia was lying naked on her couch.

"Someone was feenin," I smiled as I sat in the chair next to her.

"I guess you can say that," Alicia was rubbing her fingers up and down her clit. She opened and closed her legs, welcoming me into her pussy.

"Looks like you started the party without me." I started removing my clothes and her eyes stayed glued the bulge in my pants.

"Get over here." She took control and climbed on top of me. She licked on my neck and slowly massaged my balls in the process.

"Can I fuck you in your ass?"

"Yes babe. I love it." She inserted my dick in her tight, wet asshole

"Let me see how much." I moaned because it felt so good.

Alicia bounced up and down and side to side until we both came. We decided to make our way to her shower and we fucked again in there.

"I'm so hungry and tired," She stood in the mirror as she was blow drying her hair.

"What are your plans for tonight?" I smiled.

"I don't know. I thought about going out a little later but I'm not sure."

"I will be leaving tomorrow. So if you decide to stay home, I might come back over here and see you."

"I might stay home. Are you gone for good or will you ever be coming back?"

"My cousin will be back in a week or two but it will be longer for me. You act like you are going to miss me."

"I will, definitely miss all of this." Alicia pulled out my dick and started to lick the head.

"Don't worry, I will be back to see you... I promise."

I felt my phone vibrate in my pocket, it was Mooch.

"You gonna answer that?" Alicia asked, with my dick in her mouth.

"Yea, go easy on that thang," I moaned and she nodded.

"Sup cuz?"

"Nothing," I bit my lip.

"Uh huh. We are at Applebee's and I was checking to see if you wanted anything from here."

"Oh yea," I replied, as I tried to hold my composure. I think Alicia might be a little better at the head game than Morgan.

"Just order the chicken finger basket with fries."

"Anything else?" Mooch was trying to be funny.

"Naw nigga, bye." I hung up right before Alicia caught that nut.

"Damn girl."

"You taste so good; I think I'm staying home tonight."

"That's whassup, let me get a quick one in before I gotta go..

Chapter Twenty One

After a long night with Alicia and being woke up by Morgan, I was happy to be going home. We had settled all transactions and were packing our things into my Suburban by 10:00. Alicia leaned over the balcony as Mooch and I were loading up the car. She was wearing short shorts and a sports bra, looking very sexy.

Mooch spotted her immediately. "Dayum Cuz, who is that? I must've missed her."

"Yea, you definitely missed out on a great thang." I winked at her and she smiled.

"Ok, is she going like that?"

"She is going for me, but she might go for you too. I wish I had time to get some more of that head before we go."

"It's like that Cuz?" Mooch questioned.

"Yea, it's definitely like that and she loves it in tha ass." I felt my dick getting hard.

"I'm definitely gonna try that when I get back," Mooch licked his lips as we headed back to Morgan's.

"Be my guest fam," I stated.

Ass was just ass and it ain't no fun if my family couldn't have none.

Morgan was sulking in the kitchen. I knew she would so I had prepared myself for her bullshit.

"I'm goin' miss you," she said with her lips poking out.

"I know boo, but I will be back in a few weeks." I picked her up and carried her into her room.

"That seems like forever," she whined.

I unfastened her shorts and pulled down her panties. "Well, let me leave you with something to remember me by."

***

I gave Morgan some of this Grade-A tongue and some dick, but I knew she would still call me in an hour; thirsty chick.

Mooch did the driving back home and I was pleased to sit back and enjoy the ride.

"So you think the white chick will holla at me?" Mooch was still asking about Alicia.

"She probably will. It's not like she is the only white hoe out there." I was getting frustrated. Why was he always worried about the chicks I fucked?

"Damn cuz, you're not getting attached to that one you?" Mooch laughed.

"Be serious, I'm just saying, I don't know if she will holla at you or not."

"Yea ok," Mooch knew when to end a conversation with me.

My phone started ringing ending the conversation. It was Chante.

"Hey baby," I was happy to hear from her.

"Hey Yung, are you on the way home?"

"Yes we are and I can't wait to see you and the girls."

"We miss you too, how much longer?"

"We got about two and a half more hours to go baby." I smiled because I really did miss my family. They were my reason for hustling and they're my life.

"Ok, well I will be here; not too much I can do but lay around."

"That's all you need to do. We are going to the doctor on Monday and I don't want you to argue with me about it. Shannon told me that you are not feeling well. You need to quit that job too. I don't want anything happening to you or our son."

"We can go to the doctor and we will talk about my job when you get home, love you," she replied.

"Love you more." I hung up the phone.

"Is everything alright, Cuz?" Mooch must've seen the concern in my face.

"I'm not sure. Shannon said Chante hasn't been feeling too good."

"That pregnancy is getting to her. She did get pregnant soon after having Victoria. She probably needs to quit that job," Mooch said with concern.

"Yea, she is going to quit that job. I'm going to tell her about the moving plans in a week or so."

"I wonder what she is going to say?" Mooch coughed.

"I know, I'm sure she will be ok when she sees the new home and the great area that we will be moving into."

"What are you going to do with the house you're in now?" Mooch asked.

"I might give it to Shannon," I thought. "I know she wants a nice place and she's been tired of staying at Momma's."

"I wouldn't mind moving," Mooch hinted.

"That's cool. We are all family so I'm sure you could stay there if you want."

"That's whassup. I think I will let Marco stay at the apartment. We had a lot of memories in that apartment and it won't be the same without you."

"Awe, you goin' miss me too?"

"Shut up nigga, you know I' ma miss you, my right hand man."

Home at last, all of my trouble seemed to disappear when I drove into my two car garage. I noticed both Chante and Shannon's cars parked outside. I couldn't wait to wrap my arms around my woman and our girls.

"Yung is home." Isis ran up and gave me a big hug.

"I missed you," I picked her up and gave her a kiss on the cheek.

"I missed you too," she smiled and wrapped her little arms around my neck. I made my way into the kitchen and spotted Shannon feeding our daughter at the table.

"Look, your daddy is home."

Victoria immediately stretched her arms out for me. I gently placed Isis on the kitchen floor and grabbed my Lady Bug.

"Glad you made it back bruh," Shannon smiled and gave me a hug.

"Yeah, it feels good to be home."

"Chante is probably asleep but you better go wake her up, because she has been walking back and forth to the door for the past hour."

"I figured that, I had to drop Mooch off and make a couple stops before I got here."

I walked into my bedroom and saw my beautiful woman napping on the bed. I gently kissed her forehead and whispered in her ear.

"Yung," she sighed without opening her eyes.

"Yes baby, I'm back."

"I tried to stay up but Victor the third had other plans." She rubbed her belly.

"I know baby, how are you feeling?"

"Honestly, I feel so drained. I never felt this bad when I was carrying Isis or Victoria. Maybe it makes a difference when you are carrying a boy."

"I don't know, but we are definitely going to the doctor as soon as possible. Don't you have an appointment next week anyway?"

"Yes babe," Chante made her way to the bathroom. I watched her struggle with each step. I'm supposed to go on Thursday."

"Are you going to be alright until then, or do you think you need to go sooner than that?" I asked.

"I think I can manage. What's the difference in a couple days?"

"I just want what's best for you and our son."

"I know, I think I will be ok."

"Are you sure?" I asked again.

"I'm sure; I only have three more months to go."

"I know Babe." I kissed her and rubbed her tummy.

"This is the last one, I'm glad we are having a son. I'm either getting on some stronger birth control or I'm getting my tubes tied."

"Ok, we will be happy with the three that we have."

"Uh huh, I heard you say that when we had Victoria last year."

"I mean it this time Babe. I guess God wanted us to have another baby."

"Yes, God and you hiding my birth control pills."

"What?" I tried to act surprised.

"Yeah, it's funny how I came across these in your drawer last week. I wonder how they got there?"

I really didn't have anything to say, I did want to have more babies but I didn't know how to talk to Chante about it.

"I see that you are speechless, I think getting my tubes tied will be best. Dealing with you, I would probably end up pregnant every year," Chante said, as she put the pills back in her purse.

"I wouldn't do you like that babe," I kissed her softly on the lips.

"I'm not so sure anymore."

Chapter Twenty Two

"Wake up Yung," I heard Isis as she was tapping me on the shoulder.

"What's wrong baby girl?" I yawned and sat up in the bed.

"The baby is crying and she smells bad," Isis frowned.

I turned over and noticed that Chante was not in the bed with me.

"Ok, where is your mom?"

"She went to Grandma's with Auntie Shannon," Isis loved knowing any kind of information. "They haven't been gone that long. I wanted to stay home with you and Victoria"

I looked at the time on my phone; it was 10:00 a.m.

"Let me go check on your sister and then we can have some breakfast."

"I can help you with my sister, and I already ate breakfast," Isis smiled.

"Ok," I gave her a hug and made my way to my crying princess.

Sure enough, Victoria had left me a nice and stinky package. Isis helped me gather Mani's diaper and baby wipes; she was such a big helper.

"I'm glad that's over, it smells a lot better in here."

"Yes it does." I laughed as we made our way into the living room. I put in one of Isis' Disney movies and gave Victoria a bottle. Her big sister said she might be hungry because she ate a while ago. I felt my phone vibrate, it was my mother.

"Hello Momma," I tried to sound cheerful.

"Well, I'm glad to see that you are finally up. The rest of the world has been up for some time now."

"Ok and how are you?"

"I'm fine, but I think you need to take better care of your woman right now. Stop leaving her at home in her condition. Thank God your sister and I are around because I don't know what she would have done with these kids. She is pregnant, Victor and she needs your attention and help."

"Are these her words or your words?" I felt my blood boiling.

"These are my words because I read between the lines. I have been in her situation before, as you know. She needs you around. I know you provide financially for your family and I am proud of you for that. But Chante is having a difficult pregnancy, she stays tired too much and you just need to be around more."

"I understand Momma. I appreciate you and Shannon helping with the kids."

"It's no problem, she is family and you know I am always there for family."

"I know Momma," I smiled.

"When are you coming over here to see me?"

"I will come by today," I knew that was the real issue.

"Ok, well you make sure you do. I got mad at Shannon for not bringing the girls over here."

"Why Momma? I'm sure you haven't gone longer than a day without seeing them."

"You better know it, I love those girls and I love when they come over here. I might get Shannon to bring them over so they can spend the night."

"That's not a bad idea."

"It would give Chante and I some time alone."

"Yea, don't go planning any new babies after she drops this son of yours."

"I know Momma; we already agreed that three was enough."

"You know I love my grandbabies, but I want Chante to be healthy too."

"I know Momma," I smiled as I looked at Isis and her sister playing with each other.

"Is that Grandma?" Isis ran towards the phone.

"Yes it is. Did you want to speak to her?"

"Is that Isis asking for me? Put her on speakerphone."

I sat the phone in front of the girls.

"Hi Grandma," Isis danced around the phone.

"Good morning sweetheart and how are you doing?"

"I'm ok and I got to help Yung with my sister; she smelled pretty bad."

We all laughed.

"You are such a good big sister, and what is my Lady Bug doing?"

"She is trying to grab the phone and eat it." Isis replied.

"Would you like to come spend the night with me tonight?" Momma asked.

"Ok, when are you coming to get us?"

"I will take you girls over there a little later," I chimed in.

"Ok, I love you all and I will see you later." Momma replied.

"What are Chante and Shannon doing?" I asked.

"Chante is sitting in the living room with April. They have become kind of close but you know how April can be. Surprisingly, she doesn't talk bad about you that much and they really seem to be getting along. Shannon went grocery shopping for me."

"Ok Momma," I stated.

"What time are you coming by?"

"I guess around six or seven if that's alright,"

"Fine with me, see you later and I love you."

"Love you too Momma."

I hung up the phone and noticed I had text messages from Morgan and Alicia. Morgan said she missed me and Alicia wanted to know when I would be back. I responded to both but given Chante's health; I really wasn't sure when I would be back. I decided to give Mooch a call and make sure everything was ok with him and Marco.

"Whassup Cuz?" Mooch answered.

"I'm good, happy to be home." I said, as I looked at my girls.

"I know what you mean. I got my son over here with me today."

"Awe," I laughed.

"Yea, so whassup?"

"Nothing, just wanted to make sure everything is still going according to plan."

"Oh yea, Marco is really looking forward to the trip. Don't worry about a thang fam. We got this under control. How is Chante doing?"

"That's great. She is really having a tough time. I might need Marco to step in an extra time for me. I will go with Chante to her appointment and let you know what's going on."

"Alright fam, just keep me posted."

"You know I will."

With my mind a little more at ease, I spent the next couple hours enjoying my girls. We watched movies, ate some junk food and I let Isis go outside and play on her jungle-gym. It wasn't long before the two girls were ready for a much needed nap.

When I had the girls down for their nap, the phone rang. It was Chante.

"Hey babe, I thought my mother had kidnapped you. When are you coming home?"

"Oh really, we are on the way now. Shannon wanted to know if you are hungry. We fixed some plates because you know your mother cooked a nice meal."

"Yes, I'm starving. The girls wore me out today. They are both taking naps and I just managed to sit down for a few minutes."

"They can be a handful and just think, we are adding another one to the bunch."

"I am looking forward to it.Now get home because I miss you."

"We will be there soon, I love you."

"Love you too."

We enjoyed a great meal and some peace and quiet, before the girls were back up. Chante was ready for her nap and I informed her that Momma wanted the girls to spend the night. I packed some clothes and toys for the girls and let my woman get her rest.

"What time are we going to Grandma's?" Isis asked.

"I told her I would bring you around six or seven," I replied.

"I could take them, I was going over there anyway."

"Really sis?" I didn't want to deal with Momma right now.

"It's no problem and it would save you a trip."

"Thanks."

"I bet."

"What time was you going over there?"

"I guess I can go around six and then I have plans of my own."

"You and your man?" I winked.

"Yes that's right. Your sister has to get her freak on too."

"That was really too much info." I frowned.

"Bruh, Let's not go there."

"Fine with me," I smiled.

"Have you talked to Chante about the M.O.V.E.?"

"Not yet," I was glad she spelled that out. I didn't want Isis saying anything to my mother until I talk to Chante because that will be some drama.

"I figured we could talk about it tonight or in the morning."

"Sounds like a plan. What are your plans for this place?"

"I really thought about letting you stay here. I know Momma is on your nerves. You wouldn't mind if Mooch was here, would you?"

"Really bruh? Mooch? I don't care; he is just a wacker version of you. I managed to deal with you my whole life, so I'm not really worried about him." Shannon jumped up and down and gave me a big hug.

"That's whassup, it really seems like everything is going good for a change."

"You say that like it's a bad thing," Shannon questioned.

"It's not that, I'm just used to fucked up shit going on. I really don't know how to deal with the positive all the time."

"Well, try to get used to it. You got a good life, good woman and a growing family. Good things are all that should be on the agenda." She patted me on the back.

196

"You are right," I put on a fake smile. I only hoped that this good streak would continue.

Chapter Twenty Three

I didn't bother waking up Chante; she seemed to be resting so peacefully. I spent the rest of the night gathering my thoughts, smoking and jacking my dick because I was stressed. I wanted everything to work out, but for some reason I wasn't sure that would be the outcome.

I decided to fix breakfast for my lady; bacon, cheese eggs and toast. I made sure I cleaned the kitchen after I was finished cooking. I tried my best to clean up the rest of the house; I really wanted Chante to rest as much as possible. She was waking up as I entered the bedroom with her breakfast.

"Good morning beautiful," I smiled as I walked over to her side of the bed and placed her breakfast tray on the dresser.

"Good morning Yung, gotta go to the bathroom."

"I will help you babe," I hated seeing her in pain.

"Thanks sweetie. I don't know why your babies love to lay on my bladder. I get so tired of going to the bathroom all the time."

"I know babe, I made you breakfast and cleaned up the house."

"Thanks babe, that was so sweet of you."

"Anything for you, my love."

"Anything?"

"Just name it," I smiled.

"Carry this baby for me," she winked as I heard her flush the toilet.

"I would if I could," I didn't know what else to say.

"I know Bae, breakfast smells good."

"I did my best, I can wait until after you eat but I did want to talk to you about something." I helped her back to the bed.

"You can talk to me while I'm eating, you know I hate surprises."

"I know," I sighed.

"So you might as well tell me since you brought it up," Chante stated as she ate.

"Ok, I want us to move. And I'm not talking about moving down the street, I mean move to another state. I want to get our family away from this whole scene. I talked to my sister, Amari and she said there are quite a few nice homes in her neighborhood. We can go look at them whenever you feel up to it."

"What brought all this about? We haven't been in this house a whole year and now you are talking about packing the kids up and moving to South Carolina. That means getting Isis enrolled in a new school and up-rooting her from the only town she knows. Not to mention my job, I did plan on going back to work at some point."

"I know all this baby and I really think it's for the best. After this run, I'm out of the game. I want us to start off fresh and new. I have saved over $600,000 and we can start a new life with that and live very well. They have a great school district in Amari's neighborhood, nice jobs there and a couple universities or colleges. I plan on going to school and getting a real nine to five job. I don't want you worrying about my safety; I'm done putting you through all that stress,"

"I hear what you are saying babe. When can we go look at houses?" She sighed.

"Really Babe?" I was shocked.

"Why do you seem so surprised? I want what's best for our family just like you do. And if moving away from here is best, so be it. We are still close enough for Isis to see her dad and his family. My family lives in South Carolina, so it's really not a problem for me. What are you going to do with this house?"

"I thought about letting Shannon and Mooch stay here. Might as well keep it in the family. If all else fails, we could always sell it, but I am pretty sure they would love to stay here."

"Well, it seems like you gave this a lot of thought."

"I really have and I think it is for the best."

"Well, maybe we can go look after my doctor's appointment. There's only one problem."

"What's that?"

"Who's going to break the news to your mother?"

Damn, I didn't think about that. Momma was probably going to flip out because she was still upset about my sister moving out of the state. She would probably pass out when I told her that I was moving my family to the same area. For the first time in a long time, I was scared.

***

Chante and I rode in silence as we made our way to Momma's house. I didn't know how to break the news to her. She was still upset with Amari for moving out of the state. I figured I could wait until the very last minute to tell her because I couldn't deal with that drama right now.

"Are you ok?" Chante caressed my hand.

"Just thinking." I put on a fake smile.

"Would you like for me to talk to your mother? I know it's going to be hard for you to tell her that we're moving. Not to mention the fact that Shannon will be moving into our old house."

"Exactly, I don't know how she will take all of that. I just wish she wasn't so dependent on us. We are all grown, why would she expect us to stay at home with her?"

"There's nothing wrong with a mother wanting to stay close to her children. I know it will be hard for us to let our babies go. Maybe she will understand if she knows it's for the best."

"I hear what you are saying, but you just don't know my momma. She will make it seem like we are all abandoning her. I really blame my father for all of this. If he hadn't hurt her so deeply, maybe she wouldn't try to hold on to us so much."

"When was the last time you talked to your father?" Chante asked.

"It's been a while. I see him every now and then."

"Maybe you should talk to him and let him know how you feel. Maybe if he talks to your mom, she will be more understanding about her kids moving on with their lives."

"I dunno, I really don't know what to say to him."

"I could go with you if you want; I think your parents need to settle their differences and maybe that will bring peace to your family."

"I would love for us all to sit down to dinner. Amari hasn't spoken to Daddy since he left our mom for some chick across town. He is still with her and they have two sons together."

"Do you ever see your brothers?"

"From time to time, me, Shannon and April have met them and they seem alright. It's just hard because I know it upsets my mom. She never really got over my dad leaving the way he did. Especially since he just went to another woman and had kids."

"Yea, I bet that is a hard pill to swallow. I don't know what I would do or how I would feel. But I would want my kids to know their brothers or sisters.

I wouldn't try to keep my kids away from their family."

"You will never know how that feels because I would never do that to my family. I never want you to feel bitter or depressed because of the mistakes I have made."

"I believe you and I know you would never do that to our family."

My stomach began to churn as I pulled into my mother's carport.

"Just relax. We don't have to say anything to her today, so just relax and act natural."

"I'm trying but my mother always tries to read my thoughts. I just don't want to hurt her."

"I know and I'm here with you. And I will go with you to see your dad. I really think that will make a difference."

"I dunno, we will see."

I knocked on the door and we stood at the side door and listening to the footsteps approaching.

"Who is it?" April yelled.

"It's me and Chante," I replied.

April unlocked the door.

"Hello all," April smiled and gave Chante a quick hug.

"Nice to see you too sis," I smiled.

"Uh huh," April rolled her eyes.

"Momma and the girls are in the kitchen making cookies."

"I thought I smelled something good from the kitchen," Chante laughed.

"Well you just help yourself," April wrapped her arm around Chante as they entered the house. April continued to roll her eyes at me.

"What's up April?" I asked.

"I hear you plan on moving close to Amari," April had an evil grin.

"Who told you that?" I was pissed because April had a big mouth.

"I ran into Mooch's baby momma and she said something about Mooch moving to your house after y'all moved. Of course I had to act as if I already knew about it. Momma is gonna be so mad. I was planning on getting a place with Rick and our son. And now you are planning on moving too? Ughh."

"It was bound to happen at some time. Momma can't expect us to all live here with her. I blame Daddy for all this."

"Yea, this is his fault." April stated. "

"Chante thinks I should get Momma and Daddy to settle their differences."

"You are kidding, right? You know Momma can't stand being in the same room with Daddy. That's just gonna make things worse."

"Well something has to give. We are her kids, not her life mates and we deserve a chance to move as far as we want. We have our own lives to live. I always admired Amari for moving when she did. It let me know that I could do it one day."

"Do what one day?" Momma walked down the hall.

"Hey Momma, just talking to April." I faked a smile.

"I see that, I just can't believe you two are not arguing or yelling at each other."

"We don't argue all the time Momma," April rolled her eyes and made her way to the kitchen.

"It may not be all the time, but I know it's at least ninety-eight percent of the time," Momma laughed.

"Did you and the girls have fun?" I hugged and kissed her.

"Yes, and we are still having fun."

"Hi Yung." Isis waved then returned to putting her cookie dough on the cookie sheets.

"Hello beautiful."

"We have been cooking all day,"

"I bet." I picked up my baby girl and she laughed and began to drool.

These were the times that I treasured the most, family time. Watching my loved one laugh, smile and get along with one another. I wished these moments were everlasting and would never end. I was really giving some thought to what Chante had suggested. Maybe I could go talk to my dad; or maybe just call him. I searched through my list of contacts and found his number. I thought about calling him when I got home.

"Why are you so quiet, son?" Momma asked.

"No reason I'm alright. I was just checking my messages." I closed the contacts in my phone and placed it back in my pocket.

"Oh really? How is my favorite nephew doing?"

Momma always assumed I was on the phone with Mooch but at that moment, that was fine with me.

"Mooch is doing fine. He has his son with him today."

Momma smiled and made silly faces with Victoria "Well that's good, maybe you are becoming a good influence over him."

"Yea, your son is finally doing something productive with his popularity."

"Don't start. Everyone is getting along and that's the way I want to keep it." Momma pointed her finger at April

"Yes Ma'am," April replied.

She knew Momma was going to be upset about all of us moving so maybe she knew it was best to just shut up.

"Momma, I'm getting sleepy." Isis said.

"Well we can head to the house if you all are ready to go." I was ready to go before anyone slipped up and mentioned anything about moving.

"Do you have to leave so soon? We still have some cookies in the oven." Momma frowned.

"It is getting kind of late. I got a couple of things I need to take care of before it gets too late."

"I'm sure we will be back tomorrow or the next day," Chante chimed in as she picked up the kids' toys

"I will grab those. Go on and head to the car and I will get all of the girls things."

"Ok babe," Chante stood to her feet.

The children said their goodbyes to my mom and sister as they went to the car with Chante. I could tell that my mom was disappointed, but I reassured her that we would be back soon.

"I think that went well," Chante stated, as she fastened her seatbelt.

"Yes I guess it did, I think I'll call my daddy when we get home."

"That sounds like a great idea," Chante gave me a kiss.

"It was your idea, but thanks for always being so supportive."

"No problem, I'm, I'm always here for you."

After smoking a blunt and clearing my mind, I was finally able to dial my father's number. I don't know why I felt so nervous. Daddy and I always had a decent relationship. I'd tried to stay neutral because I didn't want to make my dad feel any more guilt than he already had.

I didn't think my dad would ever answer but by the fourth ring, he finally picked up the phone.

"Hello," Daddy cleared his throat.

"Hi Pops," I replied.

"Vic Jr.? How are you, son? Long time, no hear."

"I'm making it, Got a son on the way."

"Really? I thought Victoria was still a baby?" Daddy gasped.

"She is, but Victor the third will be here in a few months. Three months to be exact."

"That's great son, I hope you bring my grandbabies over here to see me. How are your sisters and your mom?" Daddy replied.

"Amari is doing great. Shannon is still in school. April is still April."

"And what about your mom?"

"Well, that's what I called to talk to you about."

"Why? Is she ok?" Daddy screamed.

"It's nothing like that. I was just hoping the two of you could talk and maybe settle your differences. I'm not here to judge you, I know I am not a perfect person but something has got to give. We kids are suffering for something that deals with the two of you. We all want to move and start our own lives but Momma won't let go of us. She makes us feel like we are abandoning her if we move away."

"I'm so very sorry, son." Daddy exclaimed.

"I wish I could have been a better man to your mother and a stronger father with you kids. I just didn't know how to make your mom happy. I know she is still hurt that I'm with Shelia. I have tried to tell her that the blame falls on me. I can't count how many times I have told her that I am sorry. She just doesn't want to hear it."

"Wow, I never knew that the two of you talked."

"Oh yes, we have talked. But you know your Momma, she never wants to listen. My advice to you, live your life son. You can't spend your life trying to make everyone else happy. You are no value to anyone if you don't value your own self-worth. I loved your Momma and I always will. But I just couldn't seem to make her happy. It became a second and third job. I never should have left you kids but I just didn't know how to deal."

"I know how Momma is. She is still mad about Amari moving out of state and my moving out of the house. I plan on moving close to Amari pretty soon but I don't know how to tell Momma."

"You just have to tell her. Don't beat around the bush about it because either way you will be moving. She may not like it but over time she will come around."

"I guess you are right," I said.

"You don't have a choice. Your mom might surprise you and be a little understanding."

"Maybe," I sighed.

"I'm glad you called and you should do it more often."

"Alright Pops, I will call you more often and might come to see you."

"Bring those grandbabies with you."

"Alright Daddy."

"I love you son."

"I love you too Daddy." I felt my eyes well up with tears as I hung up the phone. My dad was right, I was just gonna have to tell my mom the truth. Moving is best for my family and I hope she will grow to understand that.

Chapter Twenty Four

Talking to Daddy gave me a new burst of confidence. I felt like I could face my fears head on and really be a man. I may not like the outcome but I have to do what's best for my family and what is ultimately best for me.

I found the courage to tell Momma that we were moving after the baby was born. Of course she cried and of course she claimed she would never forgive me for leaving, but I knew she would; she had to.

As I was sitting and thinking about my new challenge, Mooch called.

"Whassup fam?"

"Nuthin much, just getting this money."

"How are things going?" I said hoping for the best because Marco had gone on the run with Mooch.

"Everything is everything," Mooch replied.

That was our code for 'plan Morgan', so I knew everything was going according to plan.

"That's whassup? When will y'all be back?"

"We on the road now. I will call you when I'm at the crib."

"Aiight then, later." I smiled as I put my phone in my pocket.

"What are you so happy about?" Chante waddled into the bedroom. Our son was really putting a strain on her body. Chante's face, legs and feet were so swollen. I don't remember her being so miserable when she was pregnant with Mani.

"Oh nothing, just talking to Mooch. Him and Marco are on the way home from that run."

"Oh ok, I will be so glad when I have this baby."

"I know babe," I gently kissed her on the cheek.

"Oh you have no idea," she breathed and rubbed her protruding belly.

"It's not that much longer." I smiled.

"Yung, are you the one carrying this baby?"

I didn't respond. I could see that she was in a lot of pain. The doctor expected our son to be a premature birth because of all the complications Chante was having in the pregnancy.

"Can I get you anything?" I couldn't think of anything else to say.

"I'm fine right now. Can you just check on the girls?" She managed to smile even though I could tell that she was hurting.

"Of course, my love," I blew her a kiss and made my way to the living room. Isis was reading a children's book to Mani while she was sitting in her playpen. They seemed content with one another's company, so I went into the kitchen for a beer. I opened the fridge and saw there were only two Bud Lights left. I grabbed one, popped the top and took a nice gulp. I wondered what Mooch had to tell me. Did Marco make a good impression on Morgan? Was he able to fuck her while they were there? Did he get access to her phone?

I decided to give Mooch a call; I just couldn't stand it anymore.

"Sup fam?" I said with anticipation.

"Just made it back in town. We stopping to get something to eat but you can swing by the crib in about 30 minutes."

"Oh that's whassup, lata."

I decided to call Shannon, but I didn't want to leave Chante by herself with the kids because I knew she was tired. Sis said she could come by so I felt a little relief. I was just ready to know what happened on Mooch's trip. A part of me felt a little salty about Marco fucking Morgan. Even though I didn't have the right to be mad, a part of me always saw her as my property...my bitch.

"Yung, can you pop some popcorn? Me and Victoria are going to watch a movie. And you just can't watch a movie without popcorn."

"You are so right."

"Thanks Yung, I gotta go and check on my sister before she starts crying."

I shook my head and waited on the popcorn to get done.

Just then Shannon rang the doorbell.

"Can I get the door?" Isis replied.

"Yes sweetie, it's Auntie Shannon."

I could hear the girls giggling and happy to see Shannon.

"What are you messing up in Chante's kitchen?" Shannon laughed and gave me a hug.

"I'm just getting Isis' popcorn ready for her and I'm not making a mess," I smiled and took the popcorn to Isis. She and Mani were sitting on the couch with a Dora the Explorer blanket wrapped around them. My little angels were ready for their movie and popcorn.

"You ladies enjoy your movie; me and Auntie Shannon will be in the kitchen."

They nodded and I made my way back to the kitchen and sat at the table. Shannon was helping herself to some popcorn and grape Kool-Aid from the fridge.

"So whassup bruh?" she said stuffing her mouth.

"I needed to go talk to Mooch and Marco for a minute. I just didn't wanna leave Chante by herself."

"Oh ok, how is she doing?"

"Our son is really taking a toll on her. The doctor plans on inducing her labor next month. The baby will be thirty-two to thirty-three weeks so he will be fine. Chante has too much fluid building up on her and her health is in danger."

"I told you to strap it up bruh," Shannon shook her head.

"Don't start," I was getting mad.

"Don't get an attitude with me. You know she just had a baby last year, so what do you expect? Chante needed time to heal but you just couldn't use a condom or wait for her to get her pills," she said pointing her index finger at me.

"Yea ok," I didn't want to hear that shit again.

"Is she getting her tubes tied after this one?" she continued with the conversation.

"She wants to," I looked away from her.

"You act like you are against it."

"I just feel different about it, but it's her body and I gotta respect that."

"Yes you do," Shannon chimed in.

"And y'all have a daughter and soon a son. Best of both worlds, so what more do you need?"

"True," I was done with this subject. I honestly felt like we should be able to have as many kids as God blesses us with but I guess it didn't matter what I thought because I was not the one carrying the babies.

"What time are you leaving?" Shannon took a gulp of her Kool-Aid.

"In a few, I gotta let Chante know that I'm leaving, she might be asleep already."

"Oh ok, is everything okay?"

"Hopefully, Marco went on a run with Mooch. We got a plan to get Morgan out of my hair and out of my life. I'm serious about it this time; I just have too much to lose."

212

"True, I just wish you could've realized this shit a lot sooner. You know...maybe after you and Chante moved in together? Maybe after she got pregnant with Victoria? Would those have been some good times to have realized that Morgan would be trouble?"

"Man, I really don't want to get into this bullshit right now. I know I fucked up. Why do you have to keep pointing that shit out? I'm a fuck-up. Are you happy now? I said it."

"Hold on bruh," Shannon tugged on my shoulder. She had made me so mad that I got up from the kitchen table and was headed down the hall to my bedroom.

"What?" I looked past Shannon.

"I didn't mean to upset you. I just thought that by saying those things it would make your predicament more real."

"More real?" I'd raised my voice but caught myself; I didn't want to alarm Chante or the girls. "I think about that shit every day. I wake up wondering what Morgan has up her sleeve and go to bed thinking about the beautiful family I have."

"Ok bruh. Again, I am sorry for making you mad. I just want you and the rest of this house to be safe. I don't want anything bad to happen because I would have to kill that hoe."

We both looked at each other and laughed. I really did appreciate my sister's concern, but I just hate being reminded of the shit that is constantly on my mind.

"I love you too," I'm gonna go check on Chante before I go.

"Aiight bruh, I'm gonna fix some more popcorn, heat up some chicken and watch a movie with my nieces." Shannon headed back toward the kitchen

"Alright sis," I smiled, as I made my way to the bedroom.

Chante was still propped up on the bed, watching TV and talking on the phone.

I sat on the bed beside her and kissed her on the cheek.

"Ok Byron, I'll make sure she is ready tomorrow at 5 p.m..... uh huh... okay."

"Whassup Babe?"

"Nothing major. Byron wanted to get Isis for the weekend. He plans on taking her and Malcolm shopping and to Chuckie Cheese's."

"Oh aiight." I almost felt for the guy because those two will be a handful.

"Yeah I wouldn't want to be him tomorrow. At least he doesn't have to worry about Marcie ruining it."

"And why won't she be able to ruin their fun? I mean, that's usually what she does."

"Oh you haven't heard? Marcie is in the county jail for six months. Apparently Ms. Thing got caught up writing bad checks one too many times. I'm sure the mall and countless discount stores will miss her."

We both laughed. I bet Byron feels like he is king of the world since that bitch is locked up. He probably smiles, laughs and does back-flips for no reason.

"I'm gonna go over to Mooch's for a little while. Shannon is in the living room with the girls. They are eating popcorn and watching a movie." "I didn't know Shannon was here. Let me go to this bathroom for the hundredth time and go speak to her." Chante sat up and eased off the bed

"Alright Babe, I shouldn't be gone too long."

"Alright, love you."

"Love you too."

***

The ride to Mooch's crib was a long and stressful one, even though it was only a couple blocks away. I kept imagining all the possible ways that our plan could go wrong. I thought about just coming clean with Chante about Morgan. I knew that would be hell but Morgan couldn't hold anything over my head if I already told the truth. I just prayed that Mooch had some good news and I promised God I would change my ways if he allowed me to get my family away from here safely.

I pulled onto Mooch's street, turned into his apartment complex and parked next to Marco's car. I was so nervous that I dropped my car keys as I was exiting my truck and I had a hard time finding my lighter for my cigarette. I knocked on the door.

"Who is it?" Marco yelled.

"It's just me fam," I yelled back.

I heard the door unlock and saw Marco smiling.

"Whassup fam?" Marco opened the door.

"You tell me," I stated as I made my way to the living room.

"Oh it's all good," Marco gave me a pound.

"Good, that's what I wanted to hear," I breathed a sigh of relief.

"You want a beer?" Mooch emerged from the kitchen with a six-pack in his hand.

"I'm good right now. Can we stop with all the codes and someone tell me what went on?" I replied as I sat on the couch.

"It's like I said fam." Marco grabbed a beer.

"Everything is all good. Morgan was just the type of freak that you and Mooch described her to be."

"Oh yea, so what's the info?"

"Well you know I am a charming guy to begin with"

"Fam, stop playing with me!" My patience was at its max and I just wanted to know if Marco handled business or not. I really wasn't interested in the positions or times that him and Morgan fucked.

"Ok fam, after I got her drunk, I got her on video—it was her idea and the tape proves all that. She was saying stuff like I better be nice to her or she will tell her daddy that I'm not the right man for this job. So we did our thang a time or two until she passed out. I went through her phone and that girl never erased y'all's texts. I made sure I deleted all of those. I checked her photos but she didn't have any pics of you. I broke the phone and dipped it in her liquor glass, so basically she has nothing that ties her to you."

"Okay, thanks fam, you just don't know how much I have been stressing about that chic and her devilish shit. You basically saved my life."

"No problem fam, Mooch said I should have a guaranteed job once you are gone. So I guess I should be the one thanking you."

"I told you everything was going to work out. You worry too much."

"Y'all just don't know Morgan. But I guess that explains why she hasn't been texting me lately."

"Yea,sShe thinks she got drunk and broke her phone. She was crying about losing all her contacts and some mo' shit."

216

"You just don't know how happy I am right now. When are we scheduled to go back to Morgan's?" I felt so much weight being lifted off of my shoulders.

"That really depends on you fam. I told Earl I would talk to you about the next trip because your woman was having problems. So when do you think you would be able to travel?"

"Yeah man, Chante has a doctor's appointment coming up. The last time we went, the doctor said she wanted to induce her labor by her thirty-second or thirty-third week because of Chante's health. Our son will be developed enough for him to be born."

"How many weeks is she now?" Marco asked.

"She is already thirty weeks."

"Ok so that would be two weeks from now."

"You don't think that would be too much of a gap in the time? How soon did Earl want us to return up there?" I asked.

"He really didn't give a specific time or day. I would say two to three weeks because we don't want to become familiar faces in that area, you feel me?" Mooch replied.

"Yea," I agreed.

Mooch pulled out his phone and dialed a number.

"Hello, what would be a good time? Uh huh—he said at least two weeks for the baby—ok—yeah—alright."

"What did he say?" I asked.

"We goin' do it after you find out the day of your son's delivery. When does Chante go to the doctor?" Mooch asked.

"She goes on Monday; I will let you know after we leave from the doctor's office. I'm sure I can get Shannon and April to help out with the kids. How long will we be gone?"

"The usual three to four days. It really just depends on the plug and how long everything takes; maybe we can leave a little sooner."

"The sooner the better. I already talked to Amari and the realty company in her neighborhood. Sis found us a nice four bedroom three bath home for a nice price. I already wired the down payment and we just gone pack up our stuff, and call a moving company for the major stuff. I'm done with tha' hustle and I'm done with Morgan."

"That's deep fam, I never thought you would leave the game. I feel you on being there for your family, but I just thought we would all just get this bread together forever."

"Before I met Chante and had my kids," I took a gulp of my beer. "I would probably agree with you but now I just have too much to lose. None of this money and none of these hoes are worth me losing my kids or my woman."

Chapter Twenty Five

Victor DaMone the Third made his entrance into the world a little sooner than expected, a whole week earlier than the doctors had planned. Chante's blood pressure had been off the charts and too much fluid was building up in her body. They performed an emergency C-section and my boo got her tubes tied. I'm still not happy about that but what can I do? I have my woman and I have my babies that I love more than anything; so I am a happy man.

My mother was still upset about us moving, but she was definitely showing her love to the kids and Chante. Chante and Lil' Vic had to stay in the hospital a few days but they were welcomed home with a small family gathering.

I still hadn't heard from Morgan and I was so glad Marco had destroyed her phone. I was sure she had my number memorized but maybe she was just focused on Marco for the moment. He said they have been doing a lot of messaging and talking lately, I hoped it would continue. I was so ready to be done with her and after this last trip, I could fully focus on my family and not worry about that crazy chick.

I spent a lot of time focusing on my family and spending time with them. I had a son. Nothing is more precious to a man (or that's just my opinion) than to have a future 'them'; a little boy that looks like them and will one day be a better man than them. I thought a lot about my childhood and it really brought tears to my eyes. I always knew my father, but he wasn't really there for me the way I wanted him to be. When I had questions about girls, love, or just being a man; I got no answers. I had been in the blind and just taking a lot of risks and chances. I didn't want that kind of life for my son; I wanted him to know about consequences and making good decisions.

I thought about the wonderful lady that had stood by my side from the very beginning; Chante. I didn't want her to end up like my mother; a bitter and broken woman that gave up on love and tried to suffocate her children because she was afraid to let them go. Chante deserved much better than that. It never took too much to make her happy, just my being there was all she needed. So, why couldn't I just be happy with that? Why did I always seem to stray from the one person that loved me unconditionally? What was I really afraid of?

Those questions ran through my brain on a regular basis. Maybe I was just being selfish, I had wanted what I wanted and didn't think about any consequences. I had never allowed a woman to get that close to my heart so I didn't care about their feelings. I was just heartless. Maybe I didn't deserve a woman like Chante and I probably did deserve all the drama that Morgan could bring because I'd played with their hearts and their emotions.

"Bruh, are you listening to me?"

"My bad sis," I replied.

"You seemed like you checked out for a minute," she smiled as she rocked Lil' Vic to sleep.

"Whassup though?" I patted my son on his back and kissed him on his forehead.

"I was asking you about Momma," Shannon carried my son to his crib and laid him down.

"What about her?" I stood by the door with my arms folded.

"Well, she is upset about you moving, but how do you think she will handle April moving out?"

"You know the answer to that. Momma is just gonna have to let us go and let us be grown. At first I kinda liked the fact that she always wanted me around. Like I knew I could always come over there with a chick or do whatever. But to be real, that's some kiddie shit. A real man stands on his own, and has his own. She should be happy that all her kids are trying to make it and we are not in jail or in any kind of trouble."

"That's so right. Maybe one day she will change, but I seriously doubt it."

"It's sad. I talked to Daddy a while back. He said he has tried to apologize to Momma but she just won't hear it. He said he was sorry for leaving, and that he just didn't know how to make her happy. I felt him on that though, because you can't wait around for a person to make you happy; Momma needed to be happy for herself."

"Daddy really said all that? And why are you just now telling me all this?"

"I don't know, but yeah that's what he said and I believe him. Amari needs to forgive him for doing the only thing he knew to do. Yea, he should have been there more for us, but he is willing to be here now, and he wants to be a part of our lives now. I'm a father now and my kids have definitely changed me. So I forgive Daddy and I am looking forward to getting to know him as an adult and I want my kids to know their uncles and their granddaddy."

"I feel you bruh, I love Daddy and he knows that. I try to stay neutral because there are always two sides to every story. When was you planning on going to see our Daddy?"

"I was really thinking about inviting Daddy and our brothers to our new house when we move. You know, kinda like a new start and new beginnings."

"Well you know I'm down and I'm sure April will be there. I'm sure she will have plenty to say."

"April is something else, but we know her bark is a lot more vicious than her bite." We both laughed.

"Yeah, I was talking to her this morning. She would never tell you this but she is so proud of you. She said she gives you a hard time because she is showing you tough love. April thinks that Momma was always too easy with you, and she is probably right."

"Awe, I love that little heifer too, but sometimes I be wanting to strangle her ass."

We smiled and nodded in agreement as Chante came in the kitchen.

"What are you two in here smiling about?" Chante kissed me on the cheek.

"Nothing much babe," I opened the fridge and decided to heat up some leftovers.

"Just talking about April, ok, that girl is very opinionated but I still love her."

"True, very true."

Chapter Twenty Six

It was 6 a.m., and I hadn't gotten much sleep last night. The day had finally come to make one last run to Morgan's spot. My heart felt like it was in my stomach and my head was just killing me. I was tired of just lying in the bed with my eyes closed, so I got out of bed and made my way to the bathroom. After taking a long shower, I decided to check on my babies. Victoria was awake and had a stinky surprise waiting for me. After cleaning her up, I took her into the kitchen and fixed her breakfast. While Victoria was happy and eating in her high-chair, I checked on Lil Vic. He too had a stinky surprise, so I cleaned him up and gave him a bottle. Having two babies was a lot more work than I ever expected. I didn't see how single women managed by themselves.

"What you doing up so early?" Shannon yawned. She agreed to stay at the house while I was gone to help Chante with the kids.

"I couldn't sleep for real," I said, trying to burp Lil Vic.

"Yeah, it's your last run." Shannon cleaned Mani's face and hands.

"Yep, and when I get back, we are gonna start moving."

"I'm gonna miss you bruh, but I know you are doing what's best and I'm so proud of you." Shannon put Mani in her playpen and turned on some cartoons.

"Thanks sis, I appreciate you always having my back, no matter what. You better not be a stranger, you know I want you to come visit."

"No worries bruh, you know I will visit."

I tried to smile to hide the fear that was clouding my judgment. Our plan had worked smoothly, but now I had to go to Morgan's. Seeing her face to face was always a problem for me. I had to see this thing through and not buckle down like I had been doing this whole time. I had managed to go without sex for the past month with no slip-ups. I hadn't texted or called any of the usual hoes. I was trying to be a 'one woman man' and finally be faithful to Chante as she deserved.

A part of me was still afraid that Morgan would make me weak.

**

The car ride to Morgan's was the longest and most stressful ride of my twenty-seven year life. I must've smoked at least ten cigarettes and was about to fire up another one.

"Damn fam, you are over there smoking like a damn freight train."

"I can't help it fam, my nerves are so bad." I put the cigarette out.

"Fire this up; I'm telling you, we got this thing in the bag. Stop worrying about it. All you gotta do is stick to the script, and let's get this money."

"I feel you, but you know how Morgan is with me. I have never been able to shake this girl."

"I know but if you don't do it now, you never will. Is Morgan worth losing Chante? Your kids? You gotta end this thing." Mooch inhaled the smoke.

"I know."

"Have you heard from her lately?" Mooch asked.

"Naw, I guess Marco has been keeping her busy."

"Yeah, Bruh has definitely been doing his thang. He been back up to her house a couple of times, and they talk on the phone a lot. I think she might be getting serious with him."

"Oh for real?" I was shocked and a little hurt. Here I was feeling bad about ending things with Morgan, and it seemed like she had already moved on with my little cousin.

"You alright? You seem a little disappointed or something."

"I'm cool, nice to know she is moving on. This might not be a bad trip after all."

"I told you not to worry in the first place. Marco learned from the best, so he knows what to say to the ladies."

"What's that supposed to mean? I know I'm not one to talk, but Morgan ain't like all these other bitches. I do care about the girl. So I hope Marco don't end up breaking her heart because she don't deserve that."

"I don't know if he is serious about her or not. But I thought the plan was to get her away from you?"

"That was the plan. Tell Marco to go easy on this one and if he ain't really feeling her, don't break her heart. Morgan is a good person underneath all that freakiness and she deserves a good guy."

"I hear ya, I will talk to him but I think he does like her. You been dealing with Morgan for a long time, so I will let Marco know how you feel."

"That's all I'm saying, I can't be the man she needs because of all that's involved, but I would like to see her happy."

"That's understood," Mooch nodded as we entered Morgan's apartment complex. I was still a little nervous but I had to play this thing all the way out, no turning back now.

We grabbed our bags from the trunk and walked up to the door. Mooch knocked.

Morgan opened the door and waved but she was already on the phone. Maybe she was talking to Marco—why did I find myself becoming a little jealous?

"Sup Morg?" Mooch smiled as he took off his backpack and sat it by the couch.

"Sup you guys," Morgan smiled, as she hung up the phone and placed it on her kitchen counter.

"How you been?" I asked.

"I have really been good, minus the fact that I destroyed my last phone but I got a new one," she smiled and gave me a hug.

"That's whassup," I clinched up not trying to get too close to her.

"What's wrong with you aAre you ok?"

"Yea, been up all morning with my kids."

"Oh yeah, congrats on the new baby. You had a son, right?"

"Yeah that's right, how did you know?"

"My dad told me. He also said that you wouldn't be working for him anymore, is that true?"

"Yea, that's true. I'm thinking about going to college or getting a legit job. I'm trying to really be there for my family. This hustle game just ain't for me anymore."

"Well that's too bad, so I guess I won't be seeing that much of you anymore."

"That's true," I looked away but couldn't believe she was taking all of this so well. Marco must be putting it down like I was never able to or something. A part of me was a little pissed that she wasn't upset.

"Yeah, Cuz is putting up his hustle card and moving away from ya boy," Mooch lit a cigarette.

"Moving? Moving where?"

"Oh, now I have your attention? Yeah, I'm moving."

"Why do you have to move?" Morgan put her hands on her hips.

"I'm just starting new. Why does it matter, I mean, you seem pretty content over there," I pointed to her phone.

"Yeah I have met someone, but that doesn't change the way I feel about you. You should know that by now. I still wanna see you or at least run into you from time to time."

"I can't do that no more and that's one of the main reasons why I'm moving. It's not fair to Chante and it's not fair to you. So I'm starting new in a new place and I wish you and your friend the best."

"Oh, so it's like that now?" She pouted.

"Come on Morgan? What's the big deal? You happy with your new boo, so why you sweating Yung?" Mooch chimed in.

"Mooch, you stay out of this."

"Why you telling him to stay out of it? Say what's on your mind, fam." I tried to act as if I didn't know anything

"Shut up, Mooch." Morgan yelled.

"Why are you yelling? Someone better tell me something," I still played my role.

"You know I'm gonna keep it real with you. You know how you had to miss the last couple of trips?"

"Yea," I said.

Morgan stormed into her bedroom and slammed the door.

"Well Morgan has been kicking it with Marco, your replacement." Mooch winked as we walked a little closer to Morgan's bedroom door.

"What? Marco? Oh ok." I tried to sound shocked.

227

"Why did you have to tell him that? I swear Mooch; you never know when to shut up." Morgan ran out of her room in tears

"Why are you getting so upset?" I blankly looked at her.

"I thought you would be mad at me." Morgan looked down.

"Naw, I'm not mad. I'm glad you got someone to talk to. At least now I will know that you got a money-making man in your corner. Why would I be mad?"

"For real? I didn't want you to know because I thought you would be mad. Mooch said you and Marco don't really know each other but I just didn't want to risk you being mad that we hooked up."

"Naw, I'm happy for you, for real. Matter of fact, you should invite Marco up here tomorrow or something."

"What?" Morgan looked surprised.

"For real Yung, we get the fact that you are cool with everything. So can we just set up this meeting and get this money?"

"Ok, you are right. Let's get this job done so we can get back home. I got some packing to do when I get back."

Chapter Twenty Seven

I spent the next day avoiding being alone with Morgan and avoiding all of her sexual propositions. It wasn't easy turning her down because she knew all of my spots and everything that I liked. I just kept picturing my woman and my kids; their love and understanding got me through the night. A couple cold showers helped through the night as well. I was glad to hear that Alicia had moved to a different apartment complex, so I wouldn't have to be tempted by her on this trip. My left hand was my new best friend. I couldn't wait for Chante's six weeks to be over—I might have a case of 'blue balls'.

My phone lit up, and I saw Shannon was calling my phone.

"Sup?" I answered the phone.

"Sup bruh?" Shannon replied.

"Nothing much, just taking care of business," I smiled.

"I hope that's all you are taking care of."

"Really sis? Have a little faith in me. But yeah I am sticking to the plan."

"That's what I wanted to hear. Well your kids are doing good with their crazy butts."

"Watch your mouth, my kids ain't crazy." I laughed.

"Yeah ok," she laughed.

"What about Chante?" I asked.

"She is doing ok. She went shopping with April and Momma, so I am stuck babysitting your kids and April's spawn."

"Poor baby." I shook my head.

"Tell me about it, Lil' Vic is the only one that's not giving me any trouble."

"Aw," I laughed. "You are just a good auntie."

"Yea," she replied. "Y'all goin' have to stop paying me with food and get me some medication before these kids drive me nuts. I think I will wait another ten years before I even think about having a baby."

"It can't be that bad, sis." I secretly knew that it was.

"Yeah yeah. Well let me get back to these kids. Ricky and Isis are playing hide and go seek and I gotta find them."

"Ok sis, lata."

I was hoping to wrap this trip up a day early as long as the supplier was cool with that. I didn't know how long I would be able to avoid Morgan and to be honest my body was starting to grow weak.

"What are you smiling about?" Morgan rubbed the back of my neck.

"Cut it out Morgan. I was just talking to Shannon." I pushed her off of me

"Oh, your sisters never did like me."

"It's not that they don't like you. They just know that you are the boss' daughter and dealing with you is not in my best interest."

"So I guess you care what they think now? It never seemed to matter before." Morgan walked slowly in my direction

"I never had a family before." I stopped her.

"But you had a family the last time you was here, and you didn't have a problem being with me, so what changed?" Morgan pouted.

"I been feeling this way for a while now. I just gotta be a better man now, Morgan. No more fucking off with you or anyone. Plus, you got Marco."

"Fuck Marco when it comes to you. You know you are number one." Morgan put her hands on my belt.

"NO! I can't do this anymore, try to understand."

"Well I just don't believe you." Morgan licked her lips.

"What will it take for you to believe that I am done with this thing we had going? I haven't made any moves on you since I have been here. We haven't talked on the phone at all, what more do you need?"

"That doesn't mean anything. We always go through our phases where we don't talk for a while. I'm used to that."

"I'm serious Morgan." I looked her dead in her eyes.

"I really can't do this anymore."

"Hey y'all, I got the supplier on the phone. When did you want to link up?" Mooch said, as he entered the room.

"ASAP!" I replied.

Mooch walked into the guest bedroom, and Morgan continued to stare me up and down.

"It sounds good Yung, but I don't feel like things are over between us."

There was silence and then Mooch re-entered the room.

"What did he say?" I breathed.

"He said 8 a.m., would be the earliest time because he has other clients to meet this evening."

I looked at my phone, it was 8 p.m., and I really didn't know if I could stand another night in this apartment with Morgan.

"Are you sure that's the earliest?" I felt the beads of sweat forming on my brow.

"Damn! Am I that horrible to be around? You are in that big of a hurry to get back to her and those kids?" Morgan yelled!

"Morgan, why are you tripping? My cuz is just trying to close this deal and get home. Why are you taking this so personal?"

"It's not over Yung. It's just not." Morgan grabbed her purse and her keys.

She slammed her front door with such force that it knocked one of her portraits down.

"Damn Cuz," Mooch shook his head and handed me a beer.

"Yea, and you said this was going to be so easy." I said as I opened the beer and took a gulp.

***

I really got concerned when at 10:00 Morgan hadn't made it back. Mooch tried calling her but she wouldn't answer her phone. We called Marco and he said he talked to her and she seemed alright. We advised Marco to stay on the phone with her. If she was on the phone, hopefully she wasn't up to any bullshit.

"I wonder where she went." I looked puzzled.

"Man chill, Marco is keeping tabs on her. You know Morgan; she always has to be dramatic. She knew you would be concerned, so just try not to play into that shit."

"You might be right. Yeah, she is probably just trying to get my attention. But to be real, it's working and not in a good way. You heard her, she really don't believe it's over. I have told her a hundred times and she still don't believe it."

"Just keep showing her, fam," Mooch replied.

"I just don't want this thing to get any uglier than it has to," I shook my head.

"I know. What time are you going to bed? We gotta get up early so we can handle this business."

"True, it's just been hard for me to sleep lately. I been worried about being up here and worried about how Morgan was gonna act and now she is trippin'."

"I hear ya, fam," Mooch mustered.

"Call Marco and see what's up," I held my head down.

I wondered if Morgan had any Tylenol or some shit; my head was killing me. I managed to find some Advil in the medicine cabinet in her bathroom. I took three pills and washed them down with tap water. As I looked in the mirror, I saw the fear in my eyes. I was scared; scared that everything I worked for could possibly be taken from me.

"Hey Yung," Mooch yelled.

"Here I come," I made my way into the living room. Mooch was sitting on the couch with a grin on his face.

"What's up?"

"You will never believe this; Morgan is at my crib with Marco." Mooch laughed.

"What?" I shouted.

"Yea, I was just talking to Marco and I heard her in the background. She sounded like she was happy to be there. I'm sure Marco will take good care of her."

"Damn, well I guess that's whassup." I was shocked.

"Yeah, so we can get some sleep and get this money in the morning. Marco will take good care of Morgan and we can hit the road without any problems."

"Sounds like a plan. I just can't believe things went this well. No drama and Morgan is with Marco. Wait a minute, what if she decided to go to your place to cause some drama when we got back? I said I was moving and maybe she is trying to be on some drama to stop me."

"Come on fam. Even if she wanted to be on some drama, she can't. Morgan doesn't know where you live."

"True, very true."

Chapter Twenty Eight

The deal was settled by 9:15 a.m. Mooch and I stopped to eat and get some gas for the trip home. I couldn't believe how well things turned out. Maybe I was worried for nothing. Mooch called Marco and he said Morgan was taking a shower and planned on cooking some breakfast. Maybe she had moved on and maybe she just wanted to get under my skin.

"I can't believe that was our last run together," Mooch passed the swisher to me.

"Yeah fam. I gotta let this shit go. It's just not in me to do this anymore. I'm thinking more about my family and my own future. I don't want my woman worrying about me anymore, I figure I can get a good job or maybe go to college."

"I hope I find someone like Chante. I need someone to turn my life around."

"You could always go back to Marisha," I laughed.

"So you a comedian now? I love our kids but that chick is just too crazy for me to deal with. I would rather visit and pick up my kids than live in hell with that bitch."

"Alright fam," I laughed because she was a crazy chick, paranoid and the whole nine.

"Yeah you got jokes. Just be glad you didn't end up with the baby momma from hell. You got a good chick and I'm happy for you. Maybe one day I will find someone worth settling down for."

"Thanks, I'm sure you will." I smiled.

The clouds were covering the sky, I thought it was going to rain today and I hated driving in the rain. I hoped Mooch got his windshield wipers working; my cousin was the type to forget about things like that.

"Looks like rain in the forecast," Mooch turned on a little heat and the defrost.

"Do your wipers work?" I asked.

"Yeah, I got some new ones last week."

"My bad, I just wanted to know. I don't want us wrecking because I can't see in the rain."

"Yeah ok," Mooch replied, but I could tell I had hurt his feelings a little bit.

There was an awkward silence until I decided to turn on the radio. Nothing special was playing but I would rather hear music than silence. After about forty-five minutes of music, Mooch turned the radio down.

"Marco is calling me," Mooch answered his phone.

I tried not to seem that interested in the conversation because Mooch just kept saying 'uh huh' and 'for real'. I was sure he would fill me in when he got off the phone. I wondered what Chante and the kids were up to, maybe I should call them.

"What tha fuck, are you sure?" Mooch yelled.

"What?" I asked.

"Let me call you back bruh." Mooch hung up the phone.

"Marco said that Morgan had left to go grocery shopping. Well apparently that's not all she did."

"What do you mean?" I felt nauseous.

"Morgan ran into April and Chante at the grocery store. Apparently she got into it with April about Marco and your name came up."

"What do you mean my name came up?" I felt my heart sink to my stomach.

"Morgan and April were arguing because Morgan mentioned that she was talking to Marco. April called her a no-good sleaze that needed to stay away from her family. Well, Morgan didn't know that we were all related, so naturally she felt played. Chante walked away from them and supposedly Morgan

236

shouted out, 'Yeah I fucked Yung too....plenty of times.' and then Chante punched her dead in her mouth. April broke it up but they were all asked to leave the store."

"Damn! See I told you it was gonna be some shit," I yelled.

I looked for my phone and I had eight missed calls; five from Shannon and three from Chante. I was scared to call Chante, but I did.

"Hello."

"Oh now you can answer tha fucking phone? You know what, fuck you. I don't know why I thought you was gonna be any different than Byron or the rest of these stupid niggas. Yea, I didn't know you and Morgan had been fucking off for some years now. Yeah, she told all your little business. Well, I guess the joke was on me. But it's cool though, she can have you. Me and my kids will be just fine, fuck you." Chante hung up.

"Slow down fam, you goin' get us pulled over. Matter of fact, pull this car over and I will drive." Mooch yelled at me.

"Man fuck all that, I gotta get home before Chante does something stupid. She talking 'bout 'fuck me' and Morgan can have me and some other shit."

"Damn fam! I thought we had it made."

"Yeah well I guess we was wrong. But it's my fault; I never should've fucked with Morgan. You and Shannon was right from the very beginning; damn, why wouldn't I just listen?"

"Fam! Please let me drive. You are driving too fast and you know you don't have your L's right now. Just let me drive." Mooch put his arm on my shoulder.

I pulled over, but we were still about forty-five minutes away and I wasn't in the right state of mind to be driving.

"I just can't lose her fam, not like this!" I felt the tears running from my eyes.

***

I tried calling Chante back but she sent me straight to voicemail. Shannon was upset with me and kept giving me the "I told you so" speech. I was so weak and wounded that I just listened to her talk. This was all my fault. I made the decision to cheat on a great woman, a woman that didn't deserve to get mistreated. I honestly deserved whatever punishment that she planned on giving me. I couldn't be mad at Morgan because I had played with her too. I was the one to blame.

Mooch pulled up to my driveway and cut off the truck. We sat in silence for a few minutes as we looked at my front door.

"I'm scared to go in there fam,I know I deserve all this, but I don't wanna face Chante right now."

"You got to fam, you gotta ride this thing on out. You fucked up, ain't no way around it. Now you gotta man up and handle the consequences."

"Easier said than done." I looked over at him.

"Do you love Chante?" he asked.

"What kind of question is that?" I rolled my eyes and twisted my mouth.

"Do you love your kids?" Mooch asked.

"Are you serious?" I hissed.

"Ok then, go in your house and handle your business. If you love them, they are worth fighting for...no matter what."

"Yeah," I grabbed my bag from the backseat and exited out the truck.

"Call me if you need me." Mooch waved.

"It may be sooner than you think. I might have to crash at your crib."

"You know you are welcome but I'm hoping things will be ok."

"Aiight."

I watched Mooch drive away and wished that I was in the truck with him. Well, it was time for me to face the music. It was do or die; I unlocked my front door and entered my surprisingly quiet home.

"Hello," I yelled. I saw Chante's car outside, but I didn't hear the kids or even a TV playing in the background.

"I'm back here in the room," Chante replied.

I slowly made my way to the Master's bedroom; I wondered if Chante was gonna try to attack me or something. When I got to the room I saw her sitting on the bed, surrounded by used Kleenex.

"Where are the kids and Shannon?" I eased my way into the room.

"She took the kids to your mom's house," Chante patted her eyes.

"Babe I just."

"Save it," Chante interjected as she wiped her nose.

"Do you have any idea how stupid you have made me feel and look?"

"I'm sorry Chante. I really never wanted to hurt you."

"Oh really? So I guess it was ok as long as I didn't find out about it?"

"No, it was never alright."

"Really, if it wasn't alright, then why would you do this? Why would you hurt us and make it to where I can't trust you? I told you about my relationship with

Byron but you make Byron look like a fucking saint. He never had the nerve to mess with a chick that would talk shit to me. He never played me the entire time we were together. I guess I was just some kind of joke to you, some puppet you just had on a string."

"No baby, you are nothing like that. You are the greatest gift that God could ever give me. The love of my life and the mother of my children. I would die for any of you."

"But you couldn't be faithful to me," Chante cried.

"I know I was wrong but I want to change. I haven't been messing with her or anyone, all I want is you and our family."

"I just don't believe you Yung, I can't trust you." She cried.

"I promise I have changed. I know you probably hate me right now but I am willing to do anything to make things right."

"I can't even look at you right now, I feel like the past few years have been nothing but a bunch of lies. And now what am I going to do? You managed to squeeze two babies out of me. I'm worse off now than I was when I first met you." She turned away from you.

"I know hurt you, I'm so sorry from the bottom of my heart. I don't want to lose you or our kids. I'm willing to do whatever it takes."

"Whatever it takes," Chante looked in awe, she had never seen me cry before. Honestly, I couldn't remember the last time I had ever cried.

"Whatever it takes. I'm a man and I'm not afraid to cry in front of my one true love. I just want you to know how sorry I am. I want to marry you and be a good father to our kids. I don't ever wanna lose you all, I will die without you."

I buried my face in my hands and I cried a sea of tears. I wasn't afraid to express how I was feeling. I felt Chante's hand on my shoulder and soon she wrapped her arms around me. I kept crying for all the lies I told and all the pain I had caused her. I knew in my heart that I did not deserve her but I didn't want to let her go.

"Yung, I am very upset with you but we still have our kids to think about. Maybe things will be a little strained between us but we got to be there for the kids. I would never try to separate you from them."

"I don't ever want to be separated from you either," I wiped my eyes.

"Maybe in time, we can work on that."

Chapter Twenty Nine

They say that time heals all wounds but how much time does it take to mend a broken heart? It's been over a three and a half months and I can count on one hand (well maybe two) how many times Chante and I have had sex. The times that we have had sex were more so 'mercy humps' in my opinion. It was definitely not the usual love making sessions that I have become used to. A part of me wants to protest or say something but I really don't have the right to complain. I made my bed and now I guess I had to lay in it.

We've moved. At least one thing managed to run smoothly. We got a nice brick home with five bedrooms and four bathrooms. It's in the same neighborhood as my big sister, Amari, and that's cool. I missed having her around and it gives Chante someone to talk to and hang out with. Amari got Chante a job at the Honda plant where she works and she is making good money. As for me, I'm enrolled in college. I decided to take up business management. Working the typical nine to five may be okay for some people but I want to run my own business. I have all the street sense in the world, so I figured I just need to learn what it takes to successfully run a legitimate business.

Don't get me wrong, a lot of my homies gave me a lot of flack over going to school and leaving the game, but I didn't care. At some point in time you have to grow up. There's more to life than hanging out in the streets and getting that easy money. There's too much at stake and I couldn't afford to lose my family or possibly end up in jail or worse. I never had a real purpose in life before Chante or the kids. I just did what I wanted and said fuck everything else, no attachments and no regrets.

I think more about what my father told me. He said a real man puts away childish things and becomes a provider for his family. A man accepts his responsibilities and can put his pride to the side when it comes to mistakes that he has made. A real man is a role model for his kids, and a person that his children can look up to and someone to depend on when they need him. I plan on being all those things and more for my kids, so if going legit is what I have to do, that's what I plan on doing.

I liked all my classes and surprisingly they weren't that hard. I thought I was going to be one of the oldest people in my class at twenty-seven years old. In fact, there were people in their thirties and forties in my classes so I guess I don't feel so bad. I guess you are never too old to learn something new. I know I'm not supposed to be thinking like this, but there's a fine young sister in my accounting class. She's always looking at me and paying close attention to me whenever I asked questions. I have tried not to notice her, but she be wearing the hell out of those jeans. Lord, give me strength right now.

"Victor, "can you please come to the chalkboard and write the answers to questions five through ten, please?"

"Yes ma'am," I replied.

I really hated being called out on the spot, but I guess it was something I needed to get used to. I went to the board, wrote my answers and hurried back to my seat. I noticed Michelle's sexy ass eye-balling me the whole way to my seat. If I wasn't trying to be a better man, I'm sure I could pull that chick. I would have that twenty-year-old screaming and calling my name. She got a pretty set of lips on her too, I wondered what her other set looked like.

"Victor," Mrs. Brown stated.

"Yes ma'am," I said snapping out of the daze that Michelle had me in.

"Would you be interested in leading a study group for this class? Your grades are by far the best in this class," Mrs. Brown smiled.

"I'm not sure," I replied and felt a little embarrassed.

"Well," Mrs. Brown continued to smile.

"I hope you consider it because I think you would be a real asset to the class. I plan on forming four study groups and I would love for you to lead one of them."

"If you think I'm good enough," I paused and looked around the class.

"I guess I could do it."

"That's what I wanted to hear," Mrs. Brown got up from her desk and continued with her lesson plan.

We watched a video and took notes, but the whole time I was undressing Michelle in my mind. She was driving me crazy the way she was chewing on her pen. I bet she loved things in or around that mouth.

My phone started vibrating. I was glad I had it on vibrate this time. My phone went off last week and I almost got it taken from me. I noticed it was a text from Chante.

'Hope you are doing well in your classes. I just wanted you to know that I am very proud of you. Love you.'

I felt like such a dog. Here I was thinking about another woman, again. Chante was all I needed and I was so close to making another mistake.

'Thanks babe and I love you too,' I replied.

I managed to stay focused until the end of class, and was glad to be leaving that classroom and my bad thoughts.

"Hey Victor," It was Michelle.

"Yes," I replied but tried not to look directly at her fine ass.

"I'm glad you are going to be leading one of the study groups for our class. I'm definitely signing up for your group," Michelle winked and licked her lips.

"That might not be a good idea," I said honestly.

"Why?" Michelle batted her eyes.

"You know why, I feel you looking at me in class. I can't afford to get caught up with you."

"Let me guess, you got a chick, right?"

"Right," I replied.

"That's disappointing." Michelle pouted her lips.

"I guess so," I took two steps back from her. I was hard because she smelled just as good as she looked.

"I got a woman and three kids to think about. I can't waste my time checking' you."

"I hear ya. Well, there's nothing wrong with looking."

"No disrespect, but looking is causing me a lot of problems with you. So I think you might want to sign up for a different study group."

"Ok, I don't wanna make things any harder on you than they already seem." She frowned.

She must have noticed my dick was bulging through my pants; I must admit that I was embarrassed.

"Yeah," I sighed and tried to adjust my pants.

"Well, I guess I will see you in class tomorrow."

"Alright shawty." I waved and watched her walk away.

"Victor," Mrs. Brown snapped.

"Yes ma'am," I guess Michelle's sexy body had me in a trance. I hadn't realized that I was still over my desk with my face directed towards the door.

"Are you ok? you look a little lost."

"No ma'am, I'm ok."

"Well that's good to hear. I see you have seven people signed up for your study group. I'm sure you will do just fine."

"Yes ma'am," I collected my books and noticed something scribbled on my notebook.

Michelle had left her number and wrote 'study buddy' next to her name.

"See you tomorrow, Victor." Mrs. Brown smiled and looked down at her class notes.

"Ok Mrs. Brown," I replied as I tore off Michelle's number from my notebook. I wanted to throw it away but a part of me wouldn't let me. I guess I am still a work in process, fuck it.

The End

www.ingramcontent.com/pod-product-compliance
Lightning Source LLC
Chambersburg PA
CBHW061617170626
46811CB00001B/450